I0653571

Tokyo Tales

Renae Lucas-Hall is an Australian-born British novelist and writer. She has always had a passion for reading and writing stories and speaking foreign languages. In 1991, Renae graduated from university in Australia with a Bachelor of Arts degree in Japanese language and culture. She went on to live in Tokyo for two years where she taught English. Renae has continued to work with the Japanese for many years. She has also completed an Advanced Diploma of Business (Marketing).

Renae has always loved reading and writing about Japan in particular, whether it be fiction or non-fiction. Over the past twenty years, she has visited Japan many times for writing research or as a tourist. Renae's first book *Tokyo Hearts: A Japanese love story* was published in 2012. Renae donated ten per cent of her profit from the sales of this paperback from 2012 to 2014 to the Japan Society Tohoku Earthquake Relief Fund. This novel is available as a paperback and an eBook from over sixty retailers worldwide. Renae lives in Gloucestershire in the United Kingdom with her husband.

You can read more about Renae Lucas-Hall, her books and her writing at http://www.renaelucashall.com.

* * *

Yoshimi OHTANI is a popular Japanese illustrator. Yoshimi's illustrations are featured on the book cover and throughout *Tokyo Tales: A Collection of Japanese Short Stories* by Renae Lucas-Hall.

Yoshimi OHTANI was born in Tokyo, Japan in 1980. In 2005, a great desire for creation came over her and so she began illustrating and refined her passion, establishing a new style for her work using illustrator software. Yoshimi's creations combine a traditional mindset (iki) with a sense of modern Japanesque "passive demeanour" (wabi), an "elegant simplicity" (sabi), and a "classic taste" (kare). The results give fascinating characters that are a hybrid of Japanimation/manga-comics and design/artistic expression. Yoshimi's illustrations can also be found in interiors of restaurants/bars and in magazines, in video games and music videos and in designs for phone icons and cases.

You can find out more about Yoshimi OHTANI at http://ARTas1.com/yoshimi_ohtani.

Tokyo Tales

A Collection of Japanese Short Stories

Renae Lucas-Hall

Grosvenor House
Publishing Limited

Illustrations by Yoshimi OHTANI of ARTas1®

Renae Lucas-Hall is hereby identified as author of this work in
accordance with Section 77 of the Copyright, Designs and
Patents Act 1988

The book cover picture is copyright to Renae Lucas-Hall
and Yoshimi OHTANI

This book is published by
Grosvenor House Publishing Ltd
28-30 High Street, Guildford, Surrey, GU1 3EL.
www.grosvenorhousepublishing.co.uk

A CIP record for this book
is available from the British Library

ISBN 978-1-78148-745-7

....

Cover artwork by Cathy Helms www.avalongraphics.org
Cover image by Yoshimi OHTANI of ARTas1®

....

....

Contents

My Cute Kawaii Boutique

'I'm twenty-one years old and I've been working part-time for a fashion shop in Yokohama for two years but now I'd really like to work for *My Cute Kawaii Boutique*,' I told Junko, the manager of this delightful shop, during my interview in Harajuku. I was full of hope she'd approve of me as I thought about how wonderful it would be to work in such a pretty place.

Junko, the manager of *My Cute Kawaii Boutique*, looked me over slowly from head to toe. A shiver ran down the back of my neck and I rubbed my clammy palms over the top of my skirt. This was only the second time I'd ever been interviewed.

'Are you happy to work here full-time?' Junko asked.

'Full-time work would be perfect for me,' I replied.

'I need to employ someone who doesn't need to be constantly supervised. Do you think you could work in this store by yourself sometimes without any help, Kimiko-san?' Junko asked me, raising one eyebrow.

'I think I'll be able to manage just fine after a little bit of training,' I said to Junko. I licked my dry lips and hoped Junko couldn't see that my hands had started to shake.

'That's a good answer,' said Junko as she ran her eyes over my resume.

Junko asked a few more questions about my previous retail experience in Yokohama at a shop where I'd sold predictable and appropriate clothing for staid shoppers who'd always wanted to dress exactly the same as everyone else. I thought my answers were good but maybe a bit brief. The shop in Yokohama was nothing like this one. The clothes in *My Cute Kawaii Boutique* allowed for individualism and creativity. A girl could really make a statement here and channel her inner princess. I'd never feel transparent or invisible wearing the adorable outfits surrounding me. They were calling out for me to try them on as I sat answering Junko's interview questions.

Junko finally said the words I'd been waiting to hear all morning. 'I'm looking for someone reliable and honest who I can depend upon and I think you'll be perfect for the job. You can start tomorrow.'

'Wonderful!' I replied. 'Thank you so much Junko-san. I really appreciate this opportunity.'

'Just one more thing,' said Junko as she stood up. 'You can't wear what you're wearing today if you want to work here.' She shook her head from side to side as her eyes worked their way down to my black conservative pumps. I'd never been measured up like this before and I felt my cheeks flare up and my bottom lip begin to quiver. I started to feel myself perspire under my grey pinstriped suit and white silk blouse but I knew Junko was right – my look would be completely out of place in a gorgeous shop like this, which was filled with ruffles and lace. Junko's style epitomised the Gothic Lolita look. I guessed she was in her mid to late thirties but she had such an enthusiastic and energetic personality. I could see why she could relate to the much younger girls who liked to shop in Harajuku. Her black, tailored blouse with its pin tucking and embroidered details on the cuffs and her grey, ruffled bell-shaped skirt accentuated Junko's curvaceous figure and very tiny waist and I admired the way her smoky eye makeup made her look so sophisticated.

'You're just too plain. No one will walk into this shop if they see you dressed like this and your hairstyle is so conservative,' said my new manager, wrinkling her perfectly made up forehead and throwing her hands up in despair.

'I was thinking of dyeing my hair lighter and buying some long hair extensions with lots of ringlets,' I interjected. 'I'd really like to change my style and completely transform myself into the cutest *kawaii* girl in Harajuku. Once I start earning some money I'll be able to buy clothes from your shop but I'm broke at the moment . . .'

'Come with me Kimiko-san,' said Junko. 'Don't worry about being broke. I'll pay you one month's salary in advance when you start work tomorrow. Right now, let's find something for you to wear. Do you have a *kawaii* style that you prefer?'

'I really like the Sweet Lolita style,' I replied.

Junko nodded and led me to the front of the store to a rack of clothes on the left. She pulled out a sweet vintage-inspired cardigan with lots of frills on the neckline and the sleeves and a corseted cream lace dress with a fluffy layered skirt covered in small pink polka dots, similar to the display on the wire mannequin bust at the back of the shop. Next she reached down under the rack for a pair of white 18th century-style leather boots with pretty soft pink ribbon laces before we headed over to the accessories on the other side of the boutique. Junko picked up a wide peach coloured *Alice in Wonderland* type bow that she clipped onto the side of my ponytail.

'Take these clothes and go and try them on in the dressing room over there,' Junko said to me, pointing to the rear of the store. 'You can keep the bow but you must return the dress and the boots and I'd like you to wear a different outfit every time you work here. I'd also like you to buy a pair of opaque white tights tomorrow morning. You can buy them at cost price. Do you see those pretty packets of tights on the shelf with the blue and pink garters – the type that go just over the knee? They would be perfect for your outfits if you want to get the look right.'

'Thank you so much,' I replied as Junko piled the dress and the boots into my willing hands. The idea of playing dress up every day filled me with excitement.

As I pulled back a heavy ruby red velvet curtain and entered the dressing room I could see Junko greeting a confident and very glamorous, young girl at the front of the shop. I instantly recognised her *ganguro* style. She'd perfected the look with her sexy pleated tartan miniskirt, as well as her long, fluttering fake eyelashes, her lavishly curled hair, her black gel nail art accented with rhinestones, her vamped up blue contact lenses and her deep, dark fake tan.

I peeked out from behind the dressing room curtain and watched the *ganguro* girl select a hooded fleecy jacket with little bear ears attached to the peak of the hood. She shrieked with delight as she tried it on in front of Junko who very carefully pulled the hood over her tanned face to show her the full effect, while at the same time trying not to dent the piles of fake curls attached to the crown of her head. The sweet ears that stood to attention certainly increased her cuteness factor. Well and truly delighted, the *ganguro* girl admired herself in the mirror for a couple of minutes. After taking off the jacket, she was very quick to pull out her purse. Junko accepted ¥5,000 from the *ganguro* girl, placed the money in the till and passed back ¥500 as change, before she swiftly wrapped up her jacket in tissue and put it into a *My Cute Kawaii Boutique* shopping bag. Before the customer left the shop, she promised Junko she'd return on the weekend with some friends to try on a few dresses and boots, which had caught her eye. In the space of five minutes this effervescent customer had arrived, made a quick purchase and left, leaving Junko looking very content, knowing she'd just increased her till by ¥4,500. I smiled as I closed the curtain and did up the lace dress, hoping all my sales were going to be as easy as that.

After silently complimenting myself on how cute I looked, I stepped out of the dressing room and Junko, who was putting out another jacket with bear ears to replace the one she'd just sold, turned and gave me a satisfied nod of approval.

'We just received a big batch of hooded jackets with cat and bear ears. They are very popular at the moment so I'd like you to set up a window display with these when you arrive tomorrow morning at ten a.m.,' Junko said to me. 'I really think this Sweet Lolita style suits you. Do a twirl for me.'

I was quite confident for my age and I loved the way I looked all dressed up in layers of white, pink and cream lace and frills. I didn't need any more

encouragement to do a 360-degree turn, which made the layers on the skirt bounce up and down like a princess twirling in a music box. I finished the pose with my hands on my tiny waist and one toe pointed.

'Perfect!' said Junko. 'I know the shop you worked at in Yokohama probably didn't ask you to do this but we have a different way of doing promotions here in Harajuku. My daughter will be with me in the shop tomorrow morning at eleven a.m. and she loves the Sweet Lolita style as well. Her name is Mei-chan and I'd like you to walk around with her through Harajuku, mainly on Takeshita Street and present yourselves as sweet and friendly *kawaii* ambassadors for the shop. Could you hand out flyers to potential customers and recommend the *My Cute Kawaii Boutique* for one hour tomorrow afternoon after you've had a lunch break? That should be a lot of fun for you.'

'That sounds great, I can't wait,' I replied. I couldn't believe my luck. This job was better than anything I'd expected.

'We are also having a Lolita tea party here at the shop on Friday afternoon. Would you be able to help me set this up in the morning and serve tea and cakes while I show the girls our new clothing range? Twenty of my best customers will be attending. They all love the Lolita fashion style and it would be a wonderful opportunity for you to meet them. They are lovely girls and I'm sure you'll get along well with all of them.'

'I'd love to meet them,' I replied. 'The Lolita tea party sounds like a great idea.'

'Terrific,' said Junko. 'Now, before you leave today I'd like you to familiarise yourself with everything in *My Cute Kawaii Boutique*. Go ahead and take a look around.'

'Thank you,' I replied. 'I'd love to look at everything.'

I started at the front of the shop with the racks of clothes where Junko had pulled out the dress I was now wearing. I slowly went through each of the gorgeous and whimsical garments that were for sale. As I paused to admire an outfit on one of the two wire mannequin busts near the dressing room, I could imagine myself wearing nearly all of the clothes and the fact that I could wear them for free while I was working was an added bonus.

Next I checked out the accessories on the right hand side of the shop. There were all types of key chains, cell phone charms and notepads with transparent pandas and kittens printed on them, as well as stickers and hair accessories in a wide array of soft pastels and brighter bold colours.

'A lot of the tourists buy that stock,' said Junko as she watched me from the counter, pleased that I was showing a genuine interest in all the items for sale. 'That's why they are at the front of the shop. You can make lots of very quick, small sales with those and at the end of the day that adds up to quite a lot.'

Further along the aisle were purses and bags. Most of them were patched with bear, cat and panda faces or fairy tale themes. I thought that they were all incredibly sweet and I couldn't see myself having any trouble selling them. Lastly, at the back of the shop, there were craft supplies for the customers to make their own *kawaii* clothes and accessories at home.

Junko called me over to the counter. 'Would you like to wear that outfit on your way home and wear it again when you come back in the morning?' Junko asked me.

'Really!' I replied. 'Oh yes, thank you. That would be fun.'

'Good,' Junko said. 'I can show you how to do your make-up as well to complete the look if you like.'

'Yes please,' I said, clapping my hands.

Junko pulled out her make-up kit from her handbag and applied lots of thick, black eyeliner and white eye shadow to make my eyes look a lot bigger. She also rubbed some plum coloured rouge in a circular motion onto my cheeks and finally she curled my ponytail with a pair of hot tongs. I watched how she applied the makeup, giggling at how quickly she could make over my face. I now looked like a pretty china doll and I was delighted with my transformation.

I bowed twice at the door of the shop and thanked Junko profusely before I left that evening carrying my grey suit and white blouse in a plastic *My Cute Kawaii Boutique* shopping bag, marvelling at how well I'd managed to get though such a perfect interview.

'Make sure you walk up Takeshita Street on your way to the train station so everyone can get a good look at you . . . and enjoy the attention,' Junko cried out to me as I turned and bowed one more time before shutting the door to the shop and puffing up my skirt, ready to wow the crowds as I made my way to the train station.

Junko was right. As I weaved my way through the crowds on Takeshita Street, holding onto my *My Cute Kawaii Boutique* shopping bag and beaming with happiness, many people stopped and stared at me and one foreigner even took my photo. I received the same attention after I boarded the train at Harajuku Station and travelled back towards my home in Yokohama. I was sure a lot of the young girls dressed in their business suits and returning home from their offices were eyeing me with jealousy, wishing they too could look as cute and as interesting as me.

It was seven thirty p.m. when I arrived home and I could smell the inviting aroma of my mother's cooking as I made my way from the entrance of our house and into the kitchen. My mother was standing stirring a pot of curry and chatting with my father who was still in his suit. He'd obviously just returned home from work. My father saw me first when I walked into the kitchen and I laughed watching the startled expression on his face. I was pleased he didn't recognise me for a moment.

'What are you wearing Kimiko-chan?' he roared at me in disbelief. 'You look silly.'

My father shook his head from side to side as he watched me perform a playful curtsey. I felt like such an actress in these clothes. I also enjoyed watching my mother as she laughed at my father's reaction and this encouraged me to curtsey again.

'Kimiko-chan, you look gorgeous!' said my mother. 'I suppose the interview at the shop in Harajuku went well.' She stopped stirring the curry and looked me up and down with big eyes that were full of surprise but also approval.

I knew my mother would appreciate my new look. 'Yes, it went very well,' I replied as I dropped the *My Cute Kawaii Boutique* shopping bag on the dining room table. 'I'm wearing the clothes I'll be selling at my new job. I get to wear a different outfit every time I go to work.'

'Well done on finding a job Kimiko-chan! I suppose it's fine for you to wear those clothes if you're going to be making more money,' said my father with a deep sigh as he removed his plain navy tie from around his neck before carefully folded it into a neat ball and setting it down on the table in front of him.

I turned to my mother as my father picked up the *Yomiuri Shimbun* newspaper and went into the living room, rolling his eyes and shaking his head, not wanting to look my way as I pranced and posed for them.

'Do you really like this Sweet Lolita style?' I asked my mother.

'Oh, I love it,' she replied. My mother returned her gaze to the boiling saucepan full of thick brown curry bubbling on the stove. 'You look like all the young girls in the trendy magazines. I wish I was young enough to wear this fashion style,' she said to me.

'Please don't,' I said with a laugh, knowing very well my mother would never change from wearing the plain and simple clothes that she'd always preferred. My mother was in her late thirties and she was very attractive for her age. She could have easily highlighted her pretty face and slim figure by wearing brighter lipsticks or more fashionable clothes but I'd always known her to be a woman with simple tastes who never wore garish outfits or eye-catching jewellery.

'A foreigner even took my photo on Takeshita Street in Harajuku!' I said to my mother.

'Wonderful!' she replied, lowering her gaze with a maternal pride which was clearly expressed in her smile. 'My daughter could end up in a French or British magazine with this new look – how exciting!'

'Our daughter should go back to school and get herself an education so she can get a normal full-time job,' my father cried out from the living room. I realised he was only pretending to read his newspaper and acting as if he was not showing any interest in our conversation but my father would often comment on my day when I returned home in the evenings and although he was offering me advice in a tone which some people would have misinterpreted as harsh, I knew he was always guiding me with love and affection. This made me think about how lucky I was to have parents who were always genuinely interested in my life.

My mother burst into a fit of giggles. 'Your father is so old-fashioned!' she exclaimed.

My father was quite a few years older than my mother and nearly fifty years old. He was a quiet and very prim and proper man but he'd always been a caring father and it was clear to everyone that he adored my mother.

'I'm going to really enjoy this job,' I cried out to my father. 'The full-time work will mean I'll be able to give you some money every month but if you don't like seeing me in these clothes then I could move into my own apartment.'

My mother put her hand to her mouth to smother another chuckle, knowing very well how much my father loved having me at home. She'd always liked the way I stood up to him or how I sometimes liked to tease him with idle threats of leaving the family home.

'You will not move out,' said my father to me gruffly, 'until you find yourself a decent husband.'

My father would occasionally tell me that a suitable husband would be a doctor, a lawyer, an accountant or a businessman who worked for a trading company. I had no idea how I was going to find a man to marry who met these criteria. All the boys I usually met had part-time jobs and they didn't have the most serious outlook on life but as soon as I did meet someone suitable I planned to make him love me and if I could manage to do this I knew I'd be gaining the approval of my dear father.

My mother told me dinner was nearly ready and I went upstairs, changed my clothes and removed all the makeup that had given me such a cute round face and childish features. Fifteen minutes later, I returned to the dining room for dinner with my parents in a pair of plain blue jeans, a navy striped T-shirt and my face freshly scrubbed. My father looked at me with approval as I sat down at the table, pleased I was now looking more conservative, but I already missed wearing the adorable costume I'd borrowed from the *My Cute Kawaii Boutique* and I couldn't wait to get dressed up and go to work in the morning.

'Good, you're back to normal,' said my father as he began eating the curry rice dish, which my mother had prepared.

'Only until tomorrow morning,' I replied, laughing.

'Kimiko-chan, you're going to have lots of fun working for that shop in Harajuku,' said my mother.

'I know,' I replied. 'My new manager Junko-san is very nice and all the clothes and the accessories at the shop are adorable!'

I continued eating my meal in silence until I'd finished my dinner, daydreaming about all the clothes I planned to wear in the future and sell at *My Cute Kawaii Boutique*. I now felt like I was becoming someone and not just anyone. I'd always been a wallflower, someone everyone overlooked and never noticed. Now I was about to make my impact on the world and the world was going to love me for my individualism and style.

The Lucky Bar in Nihonbashi

It was the fourteenth of June and it seemed like the worst day of the year for me. Everything had turned sour for me that day. For starters, it was the beginning of the *tsuyu* rainy season in Tokyo and I'd left my umbrella on the train that morning in my rush to get to the office. Leaving my workplace at the end of the day without anything to shield me from the rain outside, I knew I looked just as pathetic now as I did when I'd arrived at my desk at eight thirty a.m.

I remembered stumbling into work after running three blocks from Nihonbashi train station to my office not long after eight fifteen in the morning with just a plastic bag covering my head to protect me from the pouring rain. I'd wiped myself down in the crowded elevator while everyone else had shoved to one side so they didn't have to rub up against my wet clothes. As I exited the lift on the eighth floor, I felt the eyes of everyone in the office upon me as if they were judging me for showing up looking like I'd been for a swim in my work clothes. I sat down in front of my PC trying to hide from and ignore the amused expressions and the snickers from the three girls who always sat next to me. The three of them had all looked annoyingly immaculate and professional despite the rain pelting down outside. As soon as I turned on my PC, I made a dash for the bathroom to fix up my hair and makeup but in the rush to leave my apartment that morning I'd forgotten to throw my mascara, hairbrush and lipstick into my handbag and I had to smooth down my hair with my fingers and rub off any remaining makeup with tissues. I wasn't naturally pretty and I looked washed out without my eye shadow, concealer, blush and lip colour but there was nothing I could do except sweep as much of my hair over my face as I could and rush back to my desk with my shoulders hunched over, sidling up against the wall on the right where there were fewer desks to avoid than if I'd walked straight through the middle of the office which would have drawn more attention to myself.

At eleven a.m. I received an unexpected text message from my fiancé telling me he had decided to move out of the apartment which we'd shared for five years and to make matters worse he also told me he was moving in with a very sweet and beautiful girl whom he had met recently when he was out drinking with his friends. When I read the message I felt all the energy inside me wash away and I welled up inside with a mixture of emotions. Sadness had hit me first coupled with pain at the thought that my fiancé Hotaka wanted to be with another woman when he was everything I'd always wanted in a man and someone who I had never stopped loving from the moment we'd first met. Next I was overcome with anger, knowing I'd tried so hard to make him love me. I spent at least an hour each day at our apartment cleaning every inch of our home and every night after work I'd taken a lot of trouble to cook his favourite meals like tonkatsu, oyakodon, nikujaga and chicken curry while he'd sat on the sofa and watched the baseball or chatted to his buddies on the phone. After about fifteen minutes of feeling positively ill, I also began to worry that at thirty-one years old, it was too late for me to start another relationship and I wasn't pretty enough to attract another man as good-looking as Hotaka. I was also very hurt that my fiancé hadn't even bothered to talk to me before now about the fact he no longer wanted to be with me and he had shown no indication when I'd left the apartment in a flurry that morning that he was planning to move out. Exhausted and exasperated that everything in my life was falling to pieces, I spent my morning doing as much work as I could at my desk as I tried to blank out my feelings and emotions.

The day had dragged on but I continued working at lightning speed to stop myself from dwelling on the fact I was now single again. I even worked through lunch and I was right in the middle of finishing off an important task and thinking to myself that at least I had a good job to go to everyday when at three p.m. everyone on our team was called in for a staff meeting. We were told all the other branch offices were doing much better than our own and our services were no longer required. My manager had said to us, without allowing any of us to question him, that this was our last day at the office before he swiftly left the room. He'd told us in just five minutes, as he stood before us looking at the ceiling to avoid any eye contact, that we would all have to finish up at the end of the day once we had tied up all our loose ends and the managers were very grateful for all the work we'd done and they were sorry they had to let us go. I was already numb from the text message from my fiancé but I felt another blow to my stomach when I heard this would be my last day at the office, and as I made my way to my desk with a few of my other colleagues, I could see they too were left dumbstruck by the news that we'd all been made redundant and we'd have to look for somewhere else to work.

With this in mind at four p.m. my mother called me to tell me she'd lost the pearl necklace which she had borrowed from me the week before and I was so overcome from everything else that day that I didn't even get upset with her. I just had to acknowledge that nothing was going to go right for me that day and I would have to accept any misfortune that came my way because there was nothing I could do to stop this wave of bad news.

At seven p.m. our team was escorted from the office building with completely artificial reassurance from our manager that we'd all been terrific employees and we would all have no trouble finding other work. The last straw for me was when the left heel on my favourite pair of pumps snapped off as I stumbled for the last time out of the reception on the ground floor of our office building. I hobbled out onto the street with tears welling up in my eyes, looking from left to right, not knowing where to go or what to do. I didn't want to return to my apartment to spend an evening alone and I knew the only thing waiting for me at home was a half-empty flat which my fiancé had just vacated and from which he would have taken everything he owned. I knew I'd have to cook a dinner for myself without the sound of Hotaka's laughter emanating from the living room while he watched the programmes he'd always enjoyed on television.

The heel on my right shoe was also loose and I snapped that off as well so I didn't have to walk unevenly as I made my way to Nihonbashi train station just after seven p.m. It was still raining outside but not as heavily as it had in the morning. The drizzle just added to my feeling of woefulness and the stifling humidity in the air made it difficult for me to breathe. I stopped to buy a cheap, clear plastic umbrella from a convenience store and I noticed my reflection in the mirror on the side of the shop. My white cotton shirt that I'd ironed so meticulously that morning was sticking to my body from the combination of heavy rain and perspiration and I looked miserable.

I was about five minutes from the train station when I passed a corner with a MOS Burger outlet on one side and a dry cleaners on the other, looking like a piece of limp seaweed thrown up by the ocean onto a soggy beach. A flashing neon sign in the alleyway before me that read "Lucky Bar" caught my eye and the warm glow and friendly laughter from inside the establishment beckoned me towards what looked like an old-fashioned bar. Deep inside me, I realised I was looking for any excuse not to return home to my empty apartment and I knew that I wanted and needed something . . . anything . . . to cheer me up.

There was a couple standing below the awning of the bar smoking cigarettes, both of them were dressed in polyester navy suits but he was wearing bell-bottom trousers and she was wearing a tight, short skirt underneath her blazer. The man looked like he was in his thirties and the woman had the lined face of an over-worked forty-five year old. They noticed me approach and I expected them to look me up and down and snigger at my downtrodden appearance but they actually seemed really nice when I noticed their friendly nods as I walked towards them. As I came closer, they looked even more welcoming and jovial as if they were having the time of their lives and they wanted everyone to share in their happiness. They both nodded at me again as I crossed the threshold of the Lucky Bar and I really appreciated the fact that they didn't frown and laugh at me. I thought to myself that maybe my luck was changing and that the Lucky Bar was an apt name for this place.

The glow of the bar inside was even warmer than the entrance although there was a musty scent that hit you for a couple of seconds when you first entered. Three young men sitting in a row at the bar, next to a lava lamp, shuffled down to make room for me to slide onto the stool at the very end. I liked the way the bar had a 1970s theme and I thought to myself that this was very inviting.

The bartender was even younger than the three men, maybe in his early twenties, and the only one dressed casually in flared jeans and a tie-dyed T-shirt with a ripped design. He stopped his friendly banter with the businessman at the end of the bar and sauntered over towards me with a charming smile which made me blush.

'What would you like to drink?' he asked as he placed a small dish of green, salted edamame soybeans in front of me.

'A glass of white wine please,' I replied. I felt something prickly brush up against my right arm but when I turned there was nothing there and I rubbed my arm wondering if I'd had pins and needles for a moment, which was strange.

I must have been tired because a large glass of pale gold wine appeared before me in the blink of an eye. The bartender placed it on a brown coaster with an image of a green three leaf clover. When I looked into the glass, it sparkled before my eyes like it contained flecks of gold. I thought it must have been the light above me reflecting in my drink. The man next to me, who seemed to know the other two businessmen very well, smiled warmly and raised his glass of Scotch to me. We both said "kanpai" at the same time. The two other businessmen followed suit and quickly added their own salutations.

One by one, I placed the edamame soybeans in my mouth and squeezed out the beans inside while I sipped from my glass of wine. The beans were incredibly delicious and the wine had a way of moving through my body as if it was slowly soothing each one of my limbs. It was incredibly comforting to sit there and feel my whole body gradually beginning to relax. Each sip from my glass of wine felt like it was removing each and every problem that I'd had to deal with earlier that day. I wanted to ask the bartender where he'd sourced the edamame soybeans and the wine but he was busy chatting with the businessman at the other end of the bar and I quickly lost the will to ask any questions. After a long and difficult day, I was relieved to feel the tensions of the day draining away and it was so nice and warm in the bar that I thought to myself this was exactly what I was supposed to be doing that evening after such a terrible day.

After what seemed like half an hour, I found myself singing along with the other businessman to a tune called *Anata ni Muchu* by the Candies, which

I remembered as being very popular a few decades ago. The wine and the music and the good-humoured people surrounding me made me feel woozy and content and it was as if time had slowed down. The bartender offered to pour me another glass of wine and I accepted his offer willingly. As I began sipping my second glass another familiar tune, *Natsu no Yuuwaku* by the Four Leaves, started playing and everyone in the bar began to sing along. I joined in and I couldn't help laughing along with the others as I fumbled my way through most of the words, but I enjoyed every moment of the sing-along. The bartender poured me a third glass of wine and I began chatting with the businessman sitting closest to me who had mutton chop sideburns. He wasn't very good-looking but he seemed incredibly interested in me. As he spoke to me, I looked directly into his eyes and I tried to make out whether he was smiling at me but it was as if there was a haze in front of his face and the bad lighting made it difficult for me to see him properly. There was a lot of cigarette smoke in the room and the lighting was dim, but I thought this was somehow comforting and this man seemed nice enough, dressed in his brown suit with its dramatically wide lapels. When I joked about how bad my day had been and I told him how silly I'd been for taking the day so seriously, he kindly reassured me, telling me not to worry so much and he made me feel completely at ease. The other businessmen joined in on our conversation as well as the barman and it struck me that they were all being incredibly friendly as they laughed at my situation in such a good-natured way and offered me such sincere words of encouragement. It wasn't long before I really began to enjoy myself.

After what seemed like a couple of hours, I was smiling, bowing and thanking everyone in the bar as I prepared to leave for my short walk to the train station, thinking to myself that it must have been getting quite late and I should head for home.

Just as I was leaving the bar all the electricity went out for a moment. I was surrounded by complete darkness and silence and a horrible scent filled the air that smelt like burning rubber, but just as quickly the lights came back on and this brought about great cheers from everyone in the bar. I made promises to all of them at the door to the Lucky Bar that I would return the following evening, and in return every one of them begged me to keep my word.

On the train home I looked at my watch thinking it must have been about ten thirty p.m. but I was surprised to see it had only just turned eight. I was sure I'd had three glasses of wine and I was surprised I'd managed to drink so much in such a short amount of time. I didn't let this worry me too much. I was feeling pleasantly inebriated and I spent most of my train journey thinking about how nice the people were who I'd met at the Lucky Bar and the extent of their cordiality as I replayed my time there that evening over and over in my mind. I was still thinking about this as I exited the train station near my home and walked to my apartment, still feeling the warm and soothing effects of the wine which I'd consumed earlier and not feeling as bad as I knew that I would have felt if I hadn't stopped at the Lucky Bar in Nihonbashi.

When I entered my empty apartment, I immediately noticed a note from my ex-fiancé on the coffee table. It was very brief and it only took me a few seconds to read it. It basically told me Hotaka had left and he was very sorry it was so sudden. I sighed and crushed the note into a ball before I threw it across the room and watched it bounce across the floorboards and land next to the television. As I pulled my futon out of the cupboard and changed for bed, I felt the wine I'd enjoyed so much earlier that evening unexpectedly run through my veins again just as strongly as it had when I'd been sitting at the bar about an hour before. I stretched out on my bed and rested my head on the pillow, hoping the warm feeling of the wine would rush through me again. Before I knew it, I was fast asleep.

The following morning, all I thought about was returning to the Lucky Bar. I spent the whole day smiling to myself as I cleaned my apartment, prepared my lunch and ironed the skirt and top I would wear that evening when I returned to the bar in Nihonbashi. I wanted to wear something that suited the 1970s theme there and I decided to wear a pair of platform shoes. I thought a couple of times about my troubles from the day before, but my interest in returning to the bar outweighed any of these depressing thoughts.

At seven thirty p.m., I stepped out of Nihonbashi train station and walked quickly towards the bar that I knew was only a couple of minutes away, but as I turned the corner and passed the MOS Burger outlet and the dry cleaners, I stopped in astonishment. Looking down the alleyway that stretched out before me there was no Lucky Bar with its neon sign – just an old homeless man sifting through the rubbish bags which were lined up against the grotty walls. On the right, where the bar should have been was a door covered in cobwebs that looked like it had been boarded up for years. I hesitated and wondered if I'd lost my way. I thought it would probably be best to question the old homeless man who looked odd yet approachable. His clothes were grubby but he didn't look hostile and his square glasses made him look fairly intelligent.

'I'm sorry to bother you,' I said, trying to be very polite so I wouldn't upset him. 'but I'm looking for a place called the Lucky Bar – I thought it was down this alleyway but I think I'm mistaken . . . Do you know this place?'

The homeless man shuffled back a little and then suddenly straightened up and gazed straight into my eyes. 'I've been living in this area for a long time,' he said. 'And yes I do know the Lucky Bar but it burnt down thirty-five years ago.' He turned away and then swung around again quickly holding his finger in the air as if he'd just had a revelation. 'I remember now – it was thirty-five years ago to this day, on the fifteenth of June . . . I also remember the regulars . . . they were such nice people.'

I was shocked and I'd started trembling a little despite the heavy humidity and the warm drizzle that was dripping down my forehead. I reached inside my bag for my umbrella. 'Oh okay, can you tell me if they rebuilt the Lucky Bar somewhere close by?' I asked the homeless man.

'No, they never did,' he replied as he quickly passed me and hurried down the alleyway. He was out of my sight before I could say anything more to him.

I thought to myself that he must have been mistaken and I turned around and walked back up the long alleyway in a daze, looking from left to right for the neon sign which had greeted me so warmly the night before. A charred brown piece of cardboard caught my eye near the wall and I bent down to take a closer look at it. It was a coaster just like the one the bartender had placed my glass of wine upon the night before with a picture of a green three leaf clover on it, but this one had a burnt corner. I picked it up and put it into my handbag wondering if what the homeless man had told me was true. I didn't believe in ghosts, but as memories of the night before came back to me it all seemed very dreamlike. The faces of the people whom I'd met at the bar as well as the bartender weren't clear in my mind now and I felt like I wouldn't even be able to distinguish their faces from anyone else if I ever met them again.

I went to another bar that evening in Nihonbashi which was very modern and completely designed in graphite and steel, hoping to revive the same reassuring feelings of comfort that I'd felt when I'd spent time with the strangers in the Lucky Bar the night before, but there were no friendly faces inside and it lacked any sort of welcoming ambiance. I only stayed for half an hour before returning to my apartment.

Before I went to sleep that night I thought about my experiences at the Lucky Bar and although it had all been eerie and inexplicable, I realised sometimes in life you can find a little bit of luck and true goodness in people when you least expect it.

Motoko's Secret

'When did you begin to suspect that your husband might be cheating on you?' Taroo Miyazaki asked Natsumi Endo. He noticed tears beginning to well up in her eyes. He didn't like asking these questions but as a private investigator it was all part of the job. Natsumi was unlike most of the ladies he had to deal with in this line of work. She might not have been the prettiest lady he'd ever met but she had an extraordinarily kind face. Taroo glanced from one end of the room to the other and thought Natsumi's home was lovely. He couldn't help but notice she really took a lot of pride in keeping it tidy and nicely furnished, yet not pretentious. Everything around him was comfortable and inviting. The blue gingham blinds in the kitchen, the plush chocolate brown rugs, the indigo coloured silk cushions on the beige linen sofa, the wooden beech dining table covered in a sky blue linen tablecloth and the matching chairs were all stylish but not extravagant. Taroo decided, after chatting with Natsumi for just over an hour, that her husband was a very lucky man to be married to such a sweet lady and such a good housewife.

'I . . . I started worrying about my husband about four months ago when he began coming home late every Thursday and Friday night,' Natsumi replied, stuttering a little. 'Up until then I always felt like I could trust him. He usually talks to me about everything but recently he's been so secretive. Sometimes I . . . .' Natsumi shook her head, unable to continue her explanation. Her bottom lip was trembling.

'Go on,' said Taroo, gently patting her arm and lowering his gaze. He needed to get as much information as possible from Natsumi if he was going to investigate this situation properly but it was never good to apply too much pressure to vulnerable clients.

Natsumi forced out a meek smile. 'Well, it's not just the fact my husband has been coming home late. He has also been acting strangely. I've noticed he sometimes stares into space with a silly grin. I've always thought myself to be quite an intuitive person but the second time I saw this strange grin, I realised my husband of nine years might very well be having an affair. . .' Natsumi said as she bit her bottom lip.

Taroo could see Natsumi was very uncomfortable talking about her husband to a complete stranger like himself and he patted her arm again compassionately.

'I'm sorry but this is really difficult for me to explain. Would you like another cup of coffee?' Natsumi asked him.

'No, I'm fine thank you,' he replied.

Taroo could have stayed here all day with Natsumi in her living room. The sun was shining through the floor-to-ceiling windows behind him and warming the back of his neck. As he took the last sip of his coffee, he patted his stomach and wished he didn't have another client to see that afternoon. 'I have a couple more questions before I leave,' he said to Natsumi. He watched her compose herself and dab the tears away from the corner of her eyes with a white lace-trimmed handkerchief. Her eyes were wide and trusting and it wasn't difficult for Taroo to talk to her. 'When would you like me to start the investigation and begin to observe your husband's movements? Also, where does he work? I'd like to find out exactly what is going on and give you some answers as soon as possible.'

'I'd really appreciate it if you could start this week,' said Natsumi. 'He works in an office building opposite Ikebukuro Station and up until four months ago I know he always left the office between six and six thirty p.m., but now I'm not sure what time he finishes. All I know is that he gets home at about eleven p.m. every Thursday and Friday night and he refuses to talk about where he's been. In the first month, I pleaded with him to be honest with me but he didn't like me doing that at all so now I just have to accept that he's never going to tell me and I'm dying inside because of it.' Natsumi's eyelashes were sparkling in the sunlight from the tears bunching up in her eyes. 'I know he works with a lot of really attractive office ladies and I'm afraid . . . .'

Taroo held up his left hand and in a stern but understanding voice he tried to stop Natsumi from going any further. Taroo always drew his conclusions from real facts and common sense. He never encouraged his clients to jump to conclusions without concrete evidence. 'Let's not get carried away,' he reassured Natsumi. 'There may be a perfectly reasonable explanation why your husband is coming home late every Thursday and Friday evening. I don't want you to worry about anything until I have some definitive answers.'

Taroo picked up his briefcase, pushed back his chair and began walking towards the entrance of Natsumi's home. She followed him to the door, almost running with short quick steps to keep up with him. She had a very short, diminutive frame and Natsumi often had to run to keep the same pace with other people. If anyone ever observed Natsumi from a distance in the park in Kichijoji, where she often went for a walk with her husband on Sundays, they'd think that she was a child running after an adult trying to play catch up because she was so small.

Taroo's parting words to Natsumi were clear and succinct. He told her it would be advantageous if she didn't mention anything about this investigation to her husband and she was to carry on as she always had for the last four months in order to not attract suspicion. Taroo explained that if her husband knew he was being followed he might change his usual habits and if that happened Natsumi would never find out what he'd been doing after work every Thursday and Friday night for the past few months.

Natsumi bowed down three times in succession to Taroo as he laced up his shoes at the door. She thanked him twice for going to so much trouble to help her with her problem and she emphasised how grateful she was as she opened the front door with a kind smile. Taroo proceeded down the garden path but he looked behind him before he reached the gate and saw Natsumi waving to him from the entrance to her home. In just over an hour at Natsumi's house, he'd developed an enormous amount of sympathy for Natsumi. He knew it was very important not to become emotionally attached to his clients but he thought to himself that it would be difficult for anyone not to feel compassion for such a nice lady who obviously loved her husband very much. During their conversation that afternoon, he'd repeatedly tried to prevent any tears or to create any unnecessary drama. He'd changed the topic a few times to talk about the weather or the upcoming cherry blossom season after some of Natsumi's answers to his questions when he'd first arrived at her home, sensing she was an emotional woman, and wanting to prevent a river of tears.

Natsumi locked the front door after Taroo had disappeared around the corner at the end of her street and made her way slowly back to the living room. Normally, she'd take the empty coffee cups straight into the kitchen and wash them after she'd had a visitor in the middle of the day, but she felt at that moment she didn't have the strength to do this. She slumped into one of the wooden chairs at the dining room table. She pushed her empty coffee cup and saucer to one side and crossed her arms in front of her directly onto the table, before dropping her head onto her hands and letting tears fall straight down onto the blue linen tablecloth. She could feel her hands trembling and her energy depleted. She tried to release all the pain and embarrassment she'd felt discussing her marital problems with a private investigator who up until a few hours ago had been a complete stranger to her.

Natsumi wanted to call her mother or her best friend Mari and talk to them about her concerns but she decided she didn't want to alarm anyone without knowing what was really happening. A few days ago she'd decided to get in contact with a private investigator instead. Natsumi knew her husband Motoko would be mortified if he found out she'd employed a detective to follow him on the nights when he arrived home late, but she knew this private investigator called Taroo would be discreet and that afternoon he'd also proved to be very professional. This offered Natsumi a lot of reassurance. Taroo had listened patiently to her explanations and suspicions and she now felt after spending just a short time with him that she could rest a little easier and not worry so much about what her husband might be doing behind her back.

Natsumi was deeply in love with her husband. He was the only man she'd ever dated and she'd enjoyed every moment of the nine years they'd spent together as husband and wife, but a few months back he'd become secretive and in turn she'd become suspicious. It was at the start of December when Motoko started to come home late and walk in their front door at about eleven p.m. on Thursdays and Fridays. The very first time this had happened, Motoko had called Natsumi at four p.m. in the afternoon and he'd told her he would not be home until very late. He'd never been a drinker and Natsumi knew his managers at work rarely encouraged their employees to join them for drinks at the end of their working day so Natsumi couldn't figure out what was happening. Every Thursday and Friday evening when Motoko finally showed up at home after his late nights, Natsumi would be there waiting for him in the living room. She could never smell alcohol on his breath, but he did look dishevelled and exhausted and sometimes she had to clean red wine off his shirts the next day when she washed his clothes.

The following Thursday evening, three days after his meeting with Natsumi, Taroo was sitting in an American style coffee shop at the forefront of Ikebukuro Station, directly opposite the entrance to Motoko's twelve storey office building. There were hundreds of people walking in and out and he had to keep his eyes peeled if he was going to catch Motoko leaving work and follow him. His keen eyes and his lengthy surveillance experience gave him the advantage and the confidence to scan the crowd and find the man who matched the photo in his right hand. He knew Motoko might leave with one of the young office ladies or with a few of his colleagues and if he was with someone else or in a group he might be difficult to spot. Taroo was always alert and ready to tackle every unusual situation in his game of cat and mouse. He was proud of his past successes and he was well-known in his profession for his thoroughness and his ability to get conclusive results for his clients.

At exactly five forty-two p.m., a man in a blue suit and grey tie with a short haircut and a premature bald patch on the top of his head exited the office building opposite where Taroo was sitting in the coffee shop. The private investigator quickly glanced at the photo in his hand and concluded that this was definitely Motoko. He jumped up from the booth where he'd been sitting for about fifty minutes, gathered up his notes and rushed out onto the street, knowing he had to move fast if he was going to follow Natsumi's husband. Taroo was pleased for Natsumi's sake that Motoko was alone and not leaving work hand in hand with another woman, but experience had taught him that cheaters often leave their workplace separately to meet up later at a bar or restaurant a long way from their office, so as not to raise suspicion from their colleagues. Taroo thought Motoko might be heading into Ikebukuro Station and when Motoko crossed the road and started heading towards him, Taroo hid behind a crowd of businessman as he stealthily watched Motoko enter the train station not far ahead of him. Taroo followed Motoko to the Yamanote line and jumped onto the same train, always keeping a distance. He watched carefully to see where Motoko would get off from behind twenty or thirty other commuters. When Motoko disembarked at Shinjuku Station Taroo was not far behind him.

Motoko walked out of the west exit at Shinjuku Station and Taroo followed him one block without being seen until he saw Motoko disappear into a bar called *Rhythm* with a large guitar painted above the entrance. Taroo stopped at the corner of an alleyway and sat down on a black plastic crate that someone had thrown out for the rubbish. He took out his notebook and started writing down some of his observations. He recorded the fact that Motoko had left his office alone and he didn't have the appearance of someone who was doing anything wrong, but he'd been in a hurry to get to where he was going. He also took out his camera and took a photo of the street where he was sitting and the front of the *Rhythm* bar.

Taroo continued to sit on the black crate until ten twelve p.m. when Motoko left the bar. The only time he left his post was when he bought a can of Boss Brazil Original hot coffee from the vending machine a few steps away from where he was sitting. When Motoko left the bar by himself, Taroo noticed that he looked from left to right a couple of times before making his way up the street towards Shinjuku Station but apart from that his subject didn't provide him with any solid evidence he was cheating on his wife or doing anything he shouldn't. Taroo would have liked to get closer to the bar that night and peer inside to see who Motoko was meeting after work for drinks but he didn't want to forfeit his anonymity and raise suspicion. From Shinjuku Station, Taroo watched Motoko take the Chūō line for his hometown of Kichijoji before he decided to call it a night and retire to his own apartment in Shinagawa.

Taroo was exhausted when he finally arrived home. He sat at his kitchen table for an hour and drank endless cups of green tea thinking about Natsumi, Motoko and the bar in Shinjuku. He didn't get to bed until one a.m. the next morning. He was frustrated he had no clear answers for Natsumi, but he was well aware it sometimes took more than a few investigations and possibly months of gathering evidence in his line of work before he had any clear results to satisfy his clients.

Taroo followed and watched Motoko leave work and go to the *Rhythm* bar every Thursday and Friday over the next two weeks. He noted that Motoko always left the office alone at about the same time to go to the *Rhythm* bar and he always walked out of the bar just after ten p.m. before heading home each night looking absolutely exhausted. Taroo knew that if he was going to find out any more about Motoko's secret life he'd have to start taking a few more risks.

After a fortnight of watching Motoko following the same pattern on Thursday and Friday nights, Taroo decided to go inside the *Rhythm* bar in Shinjuku on a Tuesday evening to gather some more information. That night, he dressed himself in a navy suit with a recording device and a hidden camera attached to a specially made jacket. He'd dyed his hair a white blonde colour which gave him an edgy look. He also wore a pair of tortoise shell Prada tinted glasses and he carried an expensive-looking tan leather briefcase. He had the look of a businessman who liked to party.

When Taroo walked into the bar there were two young girls glamorously dressed in black and white silk shift dresses sitting at the top of the bar. They were sipping champagne with a slightly inebriated man in black jeans and a dark grey polo neck sweater who looked like he was in his thirties. Both girls smiled provocatively at Taroo as he walked past them and headed to the end of the bar to take a seat. As Taroo sat down he positioned himself so the buttons on his jacket could record everyone in the bar, even the barman. It was a small establishment that could only seat eight people with a long heavy mahogany bar top running through the middle, shaped in the form of a guitar. There were black and white photos of famous musicians lining the walls and the lighting was dimmed to create a warm and relaxing ambiance.

Taroo waited for the barman to finish his flirtatious conversation with the two girls at the other end before ordering a Scotch whisky for himself. The barman looked like an honest and interesting man who enjoyed serving drinks. He had an open face and a friendly tone to his voice which was perfect for attracting customers to the bar and keeping them there. When Taroo received his drink he was happy to just sit and listen to the others as they began a conversation about Jimi Hendrix and Noel Gallagher. Although the drink had cost him just over ¥1,200, he was glad he was not sitting outside on a black plastic crate, drinking coffee from the vending machine and shivering in the cold.

After two hours of listening to the barman and his three other customers chat about musicians and the best places in Tokyo to listen to live music, Taroo decided to come back the following week for more surveillance. Just as he leant down to pick up his briefcase, he stopped midway having heard one of the girls say Motoko's name.

'Where's Motoko-san this evening?' she asked the barman in a silky high-pitched voice. 'Isn't he working tonight?'

'He only works on Thursdays and Fridays,' replied the barman.

Taroo looked up without interrupting. He was too scared to move an inch and he was worried the others might get distracted and move on to another topic.

'Motoko-san is so nice but he always looks so tired,' the other girl said as she shuffled in her seat and rearranged her silk dress to show a bit more of her thigh to the man in the polo neck sweater.

'He's working two jobs,' replied the barman. 'He works at an office in Ikebukuro during the day and for a few hours here on Thursday and Friday nights.'

'Does he owe someone a lot of money?' asked the inebriated man in his thirties, winking at the barman and encouraging him to share some juicy gossip.

'No,' replied the barman, tilting his head back and laughing. 'He wants to take his wife to Italy for their tenth wedding anniversary as a surprise. He's working here until the end of next week and then he will have saved enough money for the whole trip.'

The three other customers smiled warmly at the barman and they all agreed Motoko was a very good man and it was so nice of him to work such long hours just to take his wife overseas on a special holiday.

Taroo asked for the bill and a receipt feeling all warm and happy inside. He also thought Motoko was a very decent and admirable person.

When Taroo left the *Rhythm* bar he was thinking about how nice it was going to be to break the news to Natsumi. So often his work uncovered the most horrible and nasty secrets and lies, but on this occasion he had some delightful news to share with his client. He decided he'd call Natsumi the following morning and ask her if they could meet again at her home to review the situation. It would be difficult for him not to blurt out the good news to her over the telephone. Taroo decided he'd rather see Natsumi in person, mainly because he wanted to see the relief on Natsumi's face when he explained to her that her husband wasn't cheating. Taroo was not usually affected by his clients' distresses but Natsumi had come across as such a sincere and kind lady when she'd shared her fears with him over a cup of coffee in her well-kept living room a few weeks earlier and he truly believed she was one woman who deserved to be happy. Taroo was hoping the good news would bring out a big, bright smile on her face to replace the apprehension he'd noticed permanently scrawled across Natsumi's forehead during their first meeting.

Taroo spoke briefly with Natsumi at ten o'clock the next morning and he could hear the strain in Natsumi's voice when she agreed to meet with him at her house later that afternoon. As soon as Taroo hung up the telephone he wished he'd sounded more positive and reassuring for Natsumi's sake when he'd spoken to her, but years of controlling his emotions for his particular line of work had not allowed him to do so.

At two p.m. Natsumi opened her front door to greet Taroo. As he removed his shoes he noticed the dark circles under Natsumi's trusting eyes and he didn't like the way she kept wringing her hands together. From experience, Taroo knew this was a sign that she'd been preparing herself for bad news from the time she'd received his call earlier that day. He attempted a warm smile as they exchanged pleasantries at the door and as Natsumi guided him into the living room he could smell hot coffee brewing in the kitchen. Natsumi left Taroo for a moment before reappearing with a plate of biscuits individually wrapped in red foil and a cup of coffee on a saucer which she rattled nervously in her shaky left hand before she set it down before him.

They shared a moment where they sat looking silently at each other from across the table; Natsumi not wanting to start the conversation in the fear that she was about to receive bad news and Taroo smiling kindly at her wondering how he should break the news to her without giving away her husband's surprise.

'I've been monitoring your husband's movements now for several weeks and I have conclusive evidence that your husband is *not* having an affair,' said Taroo firmly. He paused to enjoy the short but pleasant smile which briefly passed over Natsumi's lips and he just caught the twinkle in her eyes before doubt crept back in again and Natsumi furrowed her brow.

'Your husband has been working two jobs to save up for a big surprise for you and I'm here to reassure you there is no foul play involved,' Taroo continued to explain with absolute certainty in his voice.

Again, a smile appeared on Natsumi's lips but this time the frown did not return. 'Really?' replied Natsumi rhetorically. She placed both hands over her face for a moment before looking up at Taroo with a look of relief so powerful even he felt quite moved by her reaction.

'Can you tell me about that surprise?' Natsumi asked Taroo in a meek voice, looking child-like and innocent as she made her request.

'Ah, but then it would no longer be a surprise,' replied Taroo with a laugh that gave Natsumi every indication the surprise would be very good and it would be well worth her while to hear it from her husband's lips.

Natsumi and Taroo agreed Taroo's work was now finished and complete and they filled out some paperwork that only took up a few minutes of their time before Taroo left.

As she closed the door, Natsumi fell to the floor next to the entrance and sobbed with tears of relief and appreciation that her husband was again a good man in her mind and that all her fears had been futile. After relieving herself of all the emotion, which had built up inside of her for so many weeks on end, Natsumi went about her day with a fixed smile upon her face. Natsumi told herself over and over again as she did her housework that life was good and she silently vowed never to question her husband's love again.

Homestay Hell

Kazuko was crying like never before. They were tears of exasperation and relief. She was looking forward to travelling back to Tokyo, Japan and on to her hometown of Chiba the very next day. A five and a quarter hour bus journey would take her from York to Victoria Coach Station and from there she'd ride the tube to Heathrow Airport for her All Nippon Airways flight 202, which was leaving for Narita Airport at seven thirty-five p.m. She'd already packed all her clothes and the souvenirs she'd thoughtfully purchased for her family and friends into her hard silver suitcase with its two thick black straps wrapped around it to keep everything safe. She remembered buying the suitcase with her parents after they'd finally given in and allowed her to travel to the United Kingdom. At that time her thoughts had been overwhelmed with all the images of the wonderful places she'd hoped her homestay family would take her during her six month stay in England and for such a long time she'd been looking forward to her stay in York, trips to Bath and the Lake District, the Cotswolds and Stratford-upon-Avon as well as shopping at the famous Liberty store in London – she'd always had a passion for their classic floral prints. Unfortunately for her, Kazuko would return to Japan the following evening without having visited many of these places she'd wanted to see in the United Kingdom. Her money had not stretched as far as she'd hoped and although she'd read about the history of Northern England and the many attractions on offer in the counties surrounding York and all the other famous tourist spots in the United Kingdom that she would have loved to have seen, her travel guide and their descriptions of these destinations would remain the only source of her memories of these famous places when she returned to Japan.

Kazuko had only spent a half day in Leeds following her host sisters around Harvey Nichols where they couldn't afford to buy anything, a few hours wandering around Harrogate by herself just so she could get away from York, a single morning in Manchester with her host mother who looked through Primark for summer clothes for four hours with Kazuko tagging along behind her and one full day in London for a quick visit to the Liberty shop in Regent Street where she could only afford to buy two shirts, before she spent an afternoon on a red double-decker bus touring the sights as she sat and looked around her on the upper deck listening to an audio guide in Japanese.

With sad eyes and a heavy heart, Kazuko looked around the bedroom in which she'd spent most of her time over the past six months waiting for her return to Japan. She stared hard at the faded duvet, patterned with overly large pink roses, the old pine chest that creaked every time it was opened but never when she closed it, the shaggy cream thick pile rug at her feet that she'd spent scrubbing for two hours straight on her second evening in this room trying to remove the greyish stains and the smell of moth balls and decaying cigarettes. She spent at least a minute looking at each object trying to imprint the room in her memory so as not to forget about the place where she'd learnt more about herself in the past few months than any other year of her life.

Kazuko remembered being so excited about the prospect of travelling to England and living with a British family for six months. It was all she'd talked about with her parents and her friends for so long before she'd left Japan and now looking at the well-worn rug at her feet she smiled at her own naivety. She realised her head had been filled with romantic notions. When she was fourteen years old, Kazuko had read Emily Brontë's *Wuthering Heights* in Japanese. Sometimes in Japan in the weeks leading up to her departure for the United Kingdom, she'd imagined she would be like an Asian version of the dark-haired Catherine Earnshaw. She'd actually visualised herself falling passionately in love with a boy just like the character Heathcliff. Until she'd arrived in England she could see herself wandering around the Yorkshire Moors with him but after only a few days in York, she'd realised her dreams were only false hopes and the beauty of the town was not enough to soothe the emptiness Kazuko felt locked away in her bland and uninspiring bedroom in an ugly and very old mid-terraced house, where she'd spent most of her time.

Kazuko had often wished she'd listened to her parents when at first they'd been against her travelling to the other side of the world. Unfortunately for Kazuko, her persistence had finally broken them down when she'd very eloquently pointed out the educational advantages of a homestay in England and how she'd excelled at her

English studies in Japan. Her parents had finally agreed to her request when she'd told them her English would clearly improve if she studied at the Centre for English Language Learning at the University of York.

In the last six months, Kazuko's dream of a romantic life had been shattered by a reality which she'd never expected but after begging her parents for so many months to allow her to spend time in England, she knew she would never admit to anyone in Japan when she returned that her time in the United Kingdom was anything less than fantastic. Many times, Kazuko had wanted to call her parents and beg to return home early to the loving arms of her mother and father but her pride had stopped her from making that desperate telephone call every time.

The Stone family had met Kazuko at York train station six months earlier on a cold, windy evening in mid-January. The freezing temperatures had bitten her cheeks and her lips and turned them red and sore as soon as she'd arrived in England. She remembered back to when she'd disembarked from the train onto the platform at York, tightening her scarf and lifting her collar up as she'd descended the stairs. She'd pulled her heavy suitcase behind her as she'd anxiously scanned the crowd at the exit looking for the Stone family who'd promised to be waiting there holding up a placard with her name on it. It had been very dark and dreary outside at six p.m. and Kazuko remembered trembling in fear as she stood looking from left to right for her host family at the front of the station next to the taxi rank.

Kazuko had expected a proper, well-educated and honest looking mother and father, possibly dressed in tweed holding hands with the sweetest of daughters and all of them happy to greet her with the kindest of introductions. She'd had dreams they'd all pile into a ten-year-old blue Volvo with a friendly Golden Retriever and they'd pull up at a Grade II listed property with a bathroom for each bedroom and a big country kitchen with the smell of home-baked bread drifting into a spacious living room with a huge stone fireplace. She'd hoped to eat lots of roast beef dinners with home-grown vegetables and Yorkshire puddings on the side.

Instead, Kazuko was met by a single mother called Hope and her two slovenly daughters called Faith and Charity. She was instantly shocked by their business-like approach to the host family arrangement when her host mother walked towards her and greeted her with the words: 'Hello Kazuko, I'm Mrs Stone. Don't forget you're not part of the family and you'll have to pay for the privilege of living in our home.'

The three Stone women all had dyed red hair and it was difficult for Kazuko to guess their natural hair colour. Despite the cold, they were showing a lot of cleavage and when she tried to introduce herself she had a lot of difficulty understanding their Yorkshire accent.

Dread set in as they drove for seven minutes in a beaten-up purple Mazda with a large dent in the front passenger door to their small and cramped mid-terraced house on the edge of town, next to what she would find out later was the River Ouse. Kazuko had expected they might speak a good level of Japanese but she soon discovered they could only manage a couple of greetings in her native language despite the fact four other girls from Japan had stayed with them in the past. It didn't take long for Kazuko to learn that the Yorkshire accent was very different to the London accent which she'd heard on the television in Japan. This would prove to be the main reason for her not ever being able to fully understand the English people in York throughout her stay, despite the fact she was studying English every week at the University of York.

Kazuko was completely intimidated by the three Stone women and she dared not utter a word on the way to what would be her temporary home for the next six months. She tried not to stare at the daughters Faith and Charity as they shared banter, giggled and chatted and expelled shrill screams between incomprehensible sentences while Hope Stone manoeuvred her way through the traffic and up the hill towards their home. It was as if Kazuko was not in the car at all. The only words she understood were "boys", "nightclub" and "lots of drinks". This was the first of many times Kazuko would be ignored over the next six months.

Hope Stone pulled up in front of a very drab looking house. It blended in well with the grey clouds above them that were threatening to rain down heavily and drench them in the next few minutes. Faith and Charity jumped out and Hope followed them. Hope Stone opened the boot of the car, indicating to Kazuko to pull out her own suitcase. Kazuko lifted out her luggage and set it down beside her as she looked up and down the street. She noticed none of the houses were detached and they all had the same grey dull façade as the house into which she was about to enter. Kazuko dragged her suitcase behind Faith and Charity past a rickety gate and a small garden full of weeds to the front door as Mrs Stone locked up the car. As they entered a very narrow entrance with a steep carpeted staircase leading up to the second floor directly in front of them, Kazuko unzipped her leather boots to remove them at the door but as she did so the three Stone women frowned at her and she received her first of many reprimands for taking off her shoes at the entrance to their home. The Stone family defined this as being untidy. Kazuko quickly zipped her boots back up and followed Hope up the stairs to the bedroom which had been prepared for her. It was the first time Kazuko had ever worn shoes inside someone's home and it made her feel nervous and unsure of this arrangement straight away. She checked the bottom of her shoes for dirt and vowed to herself she would remove them and change into the house slippers which she'd packed in her suitcase, as soon as she possibly could. Kazuko had been afraid she would have to share a bedroom with Faith and Charity but for the first time that evening she sighed in relief at the realisation she would have her own room and some privacy.

On that first night in this disconcerting and unsettling new house, just after Mrs Stone had told her to keep her room tidy with a cautionary wag of her finger and shut her bedroom door with a loud slam, Kazuko quickly took her boots off and sat on the edge of the bed, looking around the small space which would become her only oasis and source of comfort compared to the pandemonium which would always be there to greet her every time she went downstairs. Kazuko laid her boots carefully next to the pine chest of drawers. She pulled her heavy suitcase up onto the bed and opened it up to begin unpacking. The first thing she pulled out was a fresh and brand new pair of pink house slippers which she promptly put on. This immediately helped her feel a little bit more relaxed until Hope Stone reappeared at her bedroom door and walked in without knocking, which gave Kazuko a fright. Hope screeched "£840" as she held out her right hand, palm upturned. Kazuko was exhausted and it took her a couple of seconds to understand. "£840" said Hope Stone again, louder this time and much slower as she came closer and thrust her palm under Kazuko's chin. Kazuko nodded and took the money from her purse. She smiled up at the large and frightening Mrs Stone as she passed her the £840 but this imposing English woman's face showed no signs of extending her any form of friendship. The company that had arranged the homestay had told her she would be expected to pay this money as soon as she arrived, but as she handed the money over to Hope and watched her count the money three times before leaving, Kazuko wondered again whether this homestay situation was far more of a business arrangement than a cultural experience for the Stone family. This was the first of many times Kazuko would wish she'd researched the homestay companies on the internet a little bit more before leaving Japan. She'd been so eager to get to England that she'd signed up for the very first homestay company which she'd found on the internet. If she'd been a little bit more diligent, she would have discovered other homestay companies that would have allowed her to move if she was unhappy with her arrangement and who would have carefully chosen a much more suitable family to host her stay in England.

Kazuko sat with an open jaw, unable to move as she sat awkwardly on the edge of the bed, and listened to Hope's heavy feet pounding the stairs as she made her way back down to the kitchen where her daughters were screaming with laughter. Although Kazuko had known she would be expected to make a monthly payment for her homestay experience, she hadn't supposed it would be her first proper conversation with Hope Stone.

An hour later, after a quick meal of chicken nuggets and oven-baked chips that left Kazuko's mouth dry and made her wonder why this family enjoyed eating food which tasted like damp cardboard, the three Stone women changed into very provocative and eye-catching outfits. The three women had all adopted big hair for their outing that evening and they'd decided to change into short, shiny skirts and revealing tops underneath three tacky variations of fake leopard-skin jackets. Charity and Faith told Kazuko they were going to the pub. They'd had to say the word "pub" four times before Kazuko eventually nodded to show them she did understand what they were saying and where they were going. It didn't appear to her that they were inviting her to join them and Kazuko was relieved she would have a few hours of peace and quiet in this strange house. When they slammed the door on their way out and she'd heard the key turn in the lock, Kazuko rushed back up to her bedroom and locked the door behind her, thankful she did not have to go out with them.

Kazuko changed into a pair of flannel pyjamas which she'd been looking forward to wearing for the first time only because there was a large Totoro pattern on the front and she hoped this cartoon character which had always cheered her up when she was a child would help her to feel a bit better about being in England that night. She crawled into the single bed, which was lumpy and much softer than her bed in Japan and wrapped her arms around herself as she cowered in the foetal position under the faded duvet which smelt of moth balls.

She watched the bedroom door for hours before she fell asleep, afraid Hope, Faith or Charity might return from wherever they'd been partying that night and barge in to announce they were finally home.

The next morning Kazuko discovered Hope Stone had a key to her room when she woke up suddenly from the sound of the door rattling. She watched in alarm as the door knob turned and Hope's face appeared through the crack in the door. Mascara stains ran down Hope's left cheek and her hair was sticking out in a way that made it look like a cat had attacked her in the middle of the night. Hope screeched the word "breakfast" and Kazuko nodded as she held the top of the duvet tightly around her neck, scared that Hope was going to rush in and pull her out of the bed by her hair. Kazuko quickly jumped out of bed after Hope had left and changed swiftly into her jeans and a thick black woollen jumper, afraid that if she wasn't quick enough any of the three English women would open the door suddenly and find her standing in the middle of the bedroom, half naked. A few minutes later, Kazuko made her way downstairs with trepidation and joined Hope and her daughters at the table in the kitchen for two slices of toast with butter and jam. About forty-five minutes later, Hope, Faith and Charity Stone all went off to work at the local Greggs bakery where Kazuko would later discover, you could buy the very popular bacon, lettuce and tomato sandwich and a lot of other popular English delights for just a few pounds.

Kazuko decided to look around the house that she'd call home for the next few months and she was surprised to see the Stone family mysteriously had all the latest kitchen appliances and a large 50" flat screen television in the living room, even though they only worked part-time at the local bakery. They were obviously not a rich family but Kazuko could see they liked to fill their home with expensive, if not slightly tacky furniture and the latest technology and gadgets. Both the Stone daughters had the latest iPhones and their house was filled with large, imposing leather sofas and armchairs which reminded Kazuko of the time when she was twelve years old and a friend had given her some plastic toy furniture for her dolls' house that was much too big and looked completely out of place, but which she had to accept graciously because it was a gift. The huge television, the ornate wooden coffee table and the big leather sofas made the Stone family's tiny living room look even smaller than it actually was, just as her dolls' house had looked when she'd filled it with the oversized furniture after she'd unwrapped the present from her friend many years ago. It was as if the Stone family had piled all their accumulated possessions into a storage locker where every corner was filled to save on space. This was totally different to the minimalistic floor plan inside her home in Chiba and her friends' homes in Japan. As Kazuko made herself another piece of toast she thought to herself the living room would look much better if they replaced their big heavy sofa with cushions and sat under the coffee table instead of beside it. It would definitely have opened up the room and removed the feeling of claustrophobia which would envelope Kazuko every time she came downstairs over the next six months.

As each week passed, Kazuko's time in York was pretty much like every other week. Kazuko went to her part-time English language classes and came home to a dinner of chicken nuggets, fish fingers or sausages with a side of chips. She spent most days studying in her room or in the library at the university or wandering around York by herself. It was undoubtedly a very pretty town and for that she was appreciative but in her diary she would etch a large cross over every day that passed. The worst part of her day was when she sat at the dinner table for supper with the Stone family and she tried not to get upset as they asked her their stupid questions and laughed at her answers in broken English. They wanted to know if she had a boyfriend, if she always ate Chinese food at her home, if her clothes were all made in China and if she planned to stitch clothes in a factory when she was older. Initially, Kazuko tried to explain nervously in English that she was from Japan and her country and its customs were very different from China, but she could not get this point across and she finally gave up trying to educate the Stone family about her home country. Hope, Faith and Charity Stone had a strange way of talking but never listening. Kazuko noticed they never smiled with their eyes when they laughed in their catty and sarcastic way and she nearly always excused herself straight after dinner and rushed up to her room, preferring to spend her evenings alone.

Kazuko had met another Japanese girl called Akemi at the University of York but they'd drifted apart after a month of being friends. Akemi had the pleasure of staying with a lovely English family who lived in a very grand Georgian-style detached home on the other side of York. They had a lovely big living room with an open fireplace where Akemi's host mother upheld the tradition of serving her family and guests an afternoon tea of scones with jam and clotted cream and Twinings

Earl Grey or English Breakfast tea on Sundays. Akemi's homestay brothers and sisters had adopted her as one of the family and they took great pleasure in showing Akemi around Britain. Akemi had been to the Lake District and London several times on shopping trips, where they'd showered her with gifts of designer clothes. They'd even bought her a gorgeous classic double-breasted Burberry trench coat lined with its famous heritage Burberry plaid. Akemi had also spent a week with them in the Dordogne in France at their holiday home. Kazuko felt embarrassed and unfortunate listening to Akemi talk enthusiastically about her adventures with her homestay family and Kazuko soon found ways to avoid her new friend who had started to make her feel depressed about her own situation.

Kazuko reminded herself to be proud of the fact she'd made it through a full six months with the Stone family when she rested her head on the pillow and wiped away her tears before falling asleep for her last night in this house in York. She slept very well until the following morning. When she'd finished eating breakfast she only had to endure one more hour with the Stone family before she briefly thanked them for their hospitality and rushed off to get the bus for her journey to London before boarding her aeroplane bound for Japan. Nearly eight hours later, she'd never felt so happy when the Japanese stewardess directed her to her window seat in the middle of the All Nippon Airways aircraft and she did up her seatbelt ready for take-off.

In the future, Kazuko would never talk to anyone about her objectionable stay in the North of England. Instead, she'd describe her stay there as if she'd spent her time at Akemi's home instead. She'd tell her Japanese friends about how much she'd loved walking down the cobbled street known as the Shambles with her homestay family to buy fudge from the sweet shop and she created a story about how much she'd admired the stained glass rose window and the medieval Gothic architecture inside York Minster, where she would say her homestay mother had worked as a volunteer which wasn't true. She was always optimistic when she talked about the Stone family and her stories became more and more elaborate and generous in her descriptions every time she told them. She'd tell her friends she'd enjoyed living in a big Georgian-style home and how she used to wake up every morning to the scent of home-baked bread. She'd go into detail about all her wonderful shopping trips in London with the Stone family where they'd bought her the lovely Liberty shirts which she now owned, but of course none of this had ever really happened.

Kazuko would rave on about how kind the Stone family had been and how much she missed them now she'd returned to Japan. Kazuko would also describe to each of her friends, often with too much zeal, how she'd once happily watched the long ships race during the Jorvik Viking Festival in February in York with the Stone family and how much she'd enjoyed eating a fruity Yorkshire Fat Rascal at Bettys Café after the event with the lovely Mrs Stone and her two daughters. Her friends would smile enviously at her when she'd describe how she'd sometimes tried to feed the fat grey squirrels next to the historic ruins in the Museum Gardens in the centre of York. Kazuko also loved the way she could always hold her friends captive with stories about how the young goslings born in the first days of spring used to walk beside her protected by the older geese as she meandered her way along the River Ouse, close to the impressive Georgian-style home that belonged to the Stone family in England.

A year later, Kazuko had told her marvellous stories so many times about how much she'd enjoyed her stay in England that even she'd begun to forget the truth and before long she could no longer remember just how lonely and despondent she'd really felt during her six-month homestay in York, in faraway England.

Karin's Story

'That man is looking at you again,' said Mai.
'Which man?' Karin replied.

'The man in the grey New York Yankees sweater sitting over there on the bench. The same man who has been smiling at you for nearly a fortnight every time we walk through Tamagawadai Park after school. I think he's captivated by you!' teased Mai.

'Don't be silly Mai-chan,' said Karin. 'He's looking at everyone who walks past him. He's probably looking at us because you keep looking at him.'

'He's very good looking,' said Mai. 'I'd be flattered if he was smiling at me but he's definitely looking at you. The other day when you were walking behind me and we passed him, I turned around and saw him grinning at you not me.'

'I don't like it,' said Karin. 'It's strange that a man that age is looking at me. He looks like he's in his thirties, why would he be interested in me, do you think he realises I'm fifteen?'

Karin pulled at the hem of her pleated navy school skirt which she'd deliberately hitched up to show off her long, slim legs when she'd left her high school gate fifteen minutes earlier.

'You're blushing,' blurted out Mai as she poked Karin in the ribs. 'You do think he's attractive.'

'No, I certainly do not,' replied Karin. 'I'm embarrassed.' She wrinkled her nose in dissent at her friend Mai and ran away from her towards the park's exit gate without looking back to see if she was following her. Karin wished that Mai would stop teasing her all the time as she walked the last leg of her journey back to her home, breathing heavily and flushed from the tip of her forehead to her collarbone.

Karin and Mai had been friends for a couple of years and they'd always sat together in classes. They attended one of the best private schools in Den-en-chōfu. They were both diligent students with good grades and they were very popular with the other students. Karin and Mai were renowned for asking the teachers ridiculous personal questions in order to change the subject mid-way through a boring class, but they never pushed too much and the teachers would nearly always laugh, along with the other students, whenever the two girls joked around. Karin and Mai liked to ask the teachers what they had for lunch, what car they drove or whether they were married or had a boyfriend and usually when the classroom was in the middle of a serious discussion. The more a particular teacher hesitated to answer the question, or if the teacher began to stutter or blush, the more it would amuse the other students and they would applaud Karin and Mai for turning a dull lesson into an interesting one.

All the girls at the private school that Karin and Mai attended were envious of the way the girls at the public schools could customise their school uniforms and wear their skirts as short as they liked. Their school was very strict about how their school uniform should be worn and they knew they'd be in trouble if they were caught altering their uniform in any way. They were not allowed to wear make-up and they were often reminded that they were representatives of the private school that they attended and the way they behaved and looked was very important, whether they were inside or outside the school gates. As Karin and Mai left the school in the afternoons, they were very careful to avoid the teachers who were always on the lookout to find the students who defied them and enjoyed breaking the rules. Karin and Mai relished the idea of occasionally bucking the system and they often folded their skirts up and over at the waist to shorten the length, in the hope of impressing the boys from the other high schools in the area, before entering Tamagawadai Park on their way home.

Karin had noticed the strange man in the park staring at her every day for the last couple of weeks even before Mai had mentioned it. Now that Mai made a point of commenting on it all the time, Karin wanted to suggest that they follow a different route home. She was afraid the man, who always wore a different coloured New York Yankees sweater, would approach her and start a conversation and she didn't know how she would handle that.

When Karin arrived at the entrance to her home she was completely lost in her own thoughts about the strange man in the park who had a habit of staring at her at length. He was a tall man with thick black hair that curled up at the nape of his neck. He was neither fat nor thin, but he looked like the kind of man who would put on weight easily if he ate too much because his face was full and his cheeks were chubby. Karin thought that his blue Levi jeans fitted his long legs nicely in that the hem stopped just at the heel of his shoes and she liked his American sweaters and the casual way he dressed and leant across the park bench as he looked around him. Karin admitted to herself secretively that he was a good-looking man but she would never say it out aloud and she'd certainly never admit this to her friend Mai.

Karin took off her shoes at the entrance to her home and she glanced in to the tatami room to her right. She always did this. It had become a force of habit over the years and she just couldn't bring herself to stop doing it. She was looking for her grandmother who always used to sit in the tatami room waiting for Karin to arrive home from school, but her grandmother was no longer there to greet her. She'd passed away six months earlier and Karin missed her terribly. If her grandmother had still been alive she would have felt comfortable talking to her and only her about the weird man in the park who kept smiling at her. In the past whenever Karin used to return from school her grandmother would always be there to greet her with the sweetest smile. Karin used to sit next to her on the tatami flooring and drink green tea with her for at least thirty minutes every afternoon before she went upstairs to do her homework. Karin didn't know anyone else who came close to possessing her grandmother's patience and kind nature and she'd been the only one in her life who had seemed to really listen to her and who had always enjoyed her stories when she'd talked to her about her friends, a boy she'd liked or the latest fashions which she'd wanted to buy. Her grandmother had been old-fashioned in her style of dress in that she always used to wear one of four pretty but outdated kimonos. On the flip side, her grandmother had also been very modern in that she'd been able to help Karin with many of her teenage problems. When Karin had first starting going to school, she'd been teased for two reasons. She'd been very quiet and a little bit overweight for her age. During the first six months at the new school, the other girls had teased her about her weight and they would leave chocolate bars on her desk and later laugh at her when they had discovered her eating them in the playground. Karin had been able to talk with her grandmother about these problems and it was her grandmother's advice that had helped her to become now one of the most popular girls at school. Her grandmother had suggested likely conversations she could have with the other girls, she'd encouraged her to take up tennis and get regular exercise and she'd put delicious onigiri made with salmon or tuna and senbei rice crackers flavoured with soy sauce and mirin in her lunchbox instead of chocolates to help her lose weight. As Karin's confidence in talking with the other girls grew, she started a friendship with Mai and together they'd become an inseparable pair and now they enjoyed a reassuring popularity with nearly all of the teachers and most of the students.

As the years passed, Karin's grandmother became more and more frail and she'd sometimes asked Karin to help dress her in her kimono in the morning because of the various aches and pains, which were restricting her movement. It hurt Karin to watch the health of someone she loved so dearly deteriorate day by day until one day she came home from school to be told that her grandmother had passed away. Karin's mother had explained to her that her grandmother had died quietly and without warning and she remembered thinking at the time that it was typical of her grandmother not to cause any fuss or bother. After this day, Karin always felt a pull at her heart strings as she walked in the door after arriving home from school and an emptiness as she glanced into the tatami room. Her grandmother had been such a special person to Karin, more like a friend than an ageing octogenarian.

Karin slowly shut the partition to the tatami room until it was completely closed along with the memory of her grandmother, but only for another day. She dragged her school bag behind her as she made her way to the kitchen where her mother was listening to the radio as she prepared dinner. Her mother's long hair was swept up into a bun and as she carefully cut up some chicken on a chopping board in front of her, wisps of hair escaped in a tangle at the nape of her neck. She was wearing an apron covered in cherry blossoms that covered her clothes, her upper torso and arms completely. It was elasticised at her wrists and to an outsider her mother may have looked like a picture of domestic complacency, but after the death of Karin's grandmother her mother no longer seemed as carefree and relaxed. Despite her reassuring smiles, Karin knew her mother missed her grandmother just as much as she did.

'I'm home,' said Karin, trying to cheer up her mother with a friendly greeting.

'Welcome back,' her mother replied, nodding at her daughter before returning to the task at hand.

'What are we having for dinner?' Karin asked.

'Your favourite – oyakodon,' her mother replied with a forced smile. 'You look flustered. Are you okay Karin-chan?'

'I'm fine,' Karin said, before she turned to go upstairs to her bedroom. 'I have a lot of homework to do.'

Karin didn't have a lot of study to do but she didn't want to help prepare the dinner and she was afraid she'd mention the strange man in the park to her mother and that was one conversation she didn't want to have with her. It would probably cause her mother to worry more than she should and she knew her mother had enough of her own worries without her adding to her pile of problems.

In her bedroom, Karin threw her schoolbag under her study desk before picking up a copy of *Popteen* magazine. She flicked through it as she rested her head on her pillow, trying to take her mind off the strange man staring at her in the park. She raced through the pages of her magazine unable to concentrate. She was wondering whether it might be a good idea to talk to her mother about this man but she hesitated knowing that the man had never said a word to her. Karin didn't know what to do. She loved walking through Tamagawadai Park on her way home from school. Now that her grandmother had passed away, it was generally the best part of her day and what she looked forward to most after school. It was April and in a couple of days the three hundred cherry trees in the park would be in full bloom. Karin had been looking forward to buying snacks from Maison Kayser, the European-style bakery near the park and having a picnic under the cherry blossoms with her friends the following week. There was no way that she could ask her best friend Mai to walk another way home and avoid Tamagawadai Park.

Karin picked up a small doll that she kept propped up on her bedside table. Her grandmother had bought this for her on her fifth birthday. The doll had thick, black shoulder length hair and the face showed very little expression although it appeared to be happy. She'd called the doll Maki-chan and she knew she would treasure her forever. Maki-chan had no eyebrows, a small berry-coloured mouth turned up slightly with a sweet smile and she was dressed in a green kimono with a gold obi sash. Karin used to talk to her when she was younger and sometimes this small doll had seemed like her only friend when she'd first started at primary school in Den-en-chōfu and even nowadays she would sometimes grab her and hold her close when she needed comforting. Karin caressed the black straw-like hair and stroked the green kimono. She remembered the delight on her grandmother's face when she'd given the doll to her and the memory brought tears to Karin's eyes.

Karin had been living in her grandmother's house in Den-en-chōfu since she was four years old. It was a spacious and very charming house in a very good area and Karin had always loved living there. So many times, her grandmother had told her the story of how she and her husband, Karin's grandfather who had passed away when she was three, had moved into this large house in Den-en-chōfu after the Great Kanto Earthquake in 1923. Her grandfather had come from a wealthy family but when their home in Nihonbashi was destroyed by fire at the time of the earthquake, her grandparents had moved into this beautiful, leafy suburb of Den-en-chōfu. Her grandmother had told her how the area had been developed to emulate the garden suburbs in London and Den-en-chōfu was one of the nicest residential areas in Tokyo. Her grandmother had always told Karin she should be proud to live in such a beautiful tree-lined area and many famous people lived nearby, especially in this vicinity known as the 3-chōme area in Den-en-chōfu, which was very exclusive.

The next day, Karin and Mai were on their way home walking through the park again. Karin had been hoping all day, unable to concentrate during her lessons, that the man who dressed in a variety of New York Yankees sweaters would not be sitting in the park and she was relieved when she noticed he was not sitting on the bench where he usually sat waiting for them to pass. Karin smiled and laughed with Mai when her friend also noticed the man had disappeared. Mai joked that he was a man who only liked dating young girls and he'd met with another school girl and he was no longer interested in Karin. The two girls spent the next ten minutes joking about what kind of girl would be interested in a strange man so much older than them but just before they reached the park exit, Karin felt a tap on her right shoulder. Both girls turned around and jumped into the air a couple of inches off the ground when they saw the man in the New York Yankees sweater standing behind them. Today he had a baseball cap over the thick black hair that curled around his ears but he was still clearly recognizable to the two young girls. Both Karin and Mai screamed at the same time, looked at each other in shock and bolted down the path towards the park's exit, away from the man. They both slowed down after five minutes to catch their breath, looking behind them to see if he was racing after them but he was nowhere in sight.

'Do you think we should tell the police about that man? Why is he interested in us? He must be twice our age,' Mai said to Karin as she bent down to clutch her knees with her back heaving as she tried to catch her breath.

'I don't think that's a good idea,' Karin replied. 'He hasn't done anything wrong yet but we probably shouldn't walk through the park anymore by ourselves.'

'You're right' said Mai to Karin. 'Take care and go straight home.'

Karin nodded and broke into a run again as she left her friend who had skipped off in the opposite direction. Karin headed for her own home which was now only five minutes away.

* * *

The following day was Saturday and Karin's mother asked her daughter to go with her to the local store to buy provisions for the dinner that night. She needed Karin to help her carry home all the shopping. It was something Karin often did on the weekend and she never complained about going because she knew she could always throw a few sweets and snacks into the basket before they reached the check-out point. Now that Karin was a few years older, playing tennis on a weekly basis and a lot slimmer, she could really eat whatever she wanted without putting on weight and feeling guilty.

Karin and her mother left their house at eleven a.m. They were both in high spirits. The sun was shining and her mother looked very pretty in a mauve gingham dress which she liked to wear in the springtime. They crossed the street and Karin's mother turned to the right to take the short cut through Tamagawadai Park to the small local supermarket on the other side.

Karin knew this was the quickest and the nicest way to get to the shop and although she was afraid of walking through the park she did feel very safe and secure with her mother by her side. Karin straightened her shoulders and pushed herself forward. She thought to herself that the strange man would never bother her with her mother next to her. Her mother was not very tall but she was very strong and she had the air of a lady who didn't tolerate fools easily. Karin knew that a lot of men were afraid of her mother's assertiveness and she always felt safe when she went out with her. Karin hoped she would grow and mature to have her mother's courage and strength in the future.

Karin and her mother were talking about the forthcoming cherry blossom season, strolling casually through the park, when Karin heard a man's deep voice from behind her call out her name. Karin turned and felt her knees go weak when she recognised the strange man in the New York Yankees sweater who had frightened her and Mai the previous day.

'I can't believe it,' said Karin's mother. 'What are you doing here Daichi-kun?'

Karin looked at her mother in shock and wondered how she could possibly know the strange man from the park.

'I came to see Karin-chan,' the man called Daichi replied.

'Why does this man know my name?' asked Karin, looking back and forth at her mother's face and the strange man standing before them who was now standing very close, blushing deeply and looking at the ground, unable to look at her mother's eyes.

'Didn't you tell her about me?' the man called Daichi asked Karin's mother.

'Tell me what?' Karin asked sharply, starting to get angry with her mother and the strange man for not explaining to her what was happening.

'I'm your father,' said Daichi, matter-of-factly. He looked directly into Karin's eyes with a mixture of hope and apprehension as her pupils widened in amazement.

'My father!' said Karin who had not seen her father since she was two years old and who she'd always pictured differently in her mind. She'd always thought that her father would be about the same height as her mother and not six-feet tall like the man who stood in front of her and she'd imagined he'd be much more business-like than the man who stood before them now. Karin had also thought she'd be over-joyed when she saw her father for the first time in many years but now she just felt confused and upset.

For a couple of minutes, Karin, her mother and Daichi stared at each other in awkward silence in the middle of the park. Karin kept zipping up her white cotton jacket and unzipping it again several times. Her mother had opened up her handbag and was searching through it as if she was looking for something, but she didn't take anything out and she finally closed it for good and glared at Daichi.

'You look really well,' Daichi finally said to Karin's mother.

'I don't look well. I'm exhausted and tired but of course you look well – you haven't had the responsibility of raising a child and looking after a sick mother who for your information has now passed away,' Karin's mother replied.

'Now wait a minute – I've tried to contact you several times and you've never returned my phone calls.'

'I don't want you in our lives,' said Karin's mother.

Karin put her hand on her mother's arm when she heard the hurt in her voice and she could tell her mother was about to break into tears.

'Maybe you don't want me in your life but have you ever stopped to consider that Karin-chan might want to get to know her own father?' said Daichi.

This time it was Karin who began to cry when she heard these words and as the tears rolled down her cheeks her mother and father turned to look at her with sympathy, concern and a touch of embarrassment. Karin hadn't cried in public for many years and the shame made her cover her own face with a handkerchief which she'd taken out of the pocket of her cotton jacket.

'Are you okay Karin-chan? I'm so sorry,' her mother said to her.

'I always thought that if I ever met my father, we would all get along but this is horrible,' said Karin. She didn't take the handkerchief away from her eyes. Karin was too upset to look directly at her father or her mother.

'I'm sorry, this must be difficult for you Karin-chan,' said Daichi. 'Could I buy you both some lunch? There's a restaurant not far from here and we could all go and have something to eat.'

Karin's mother nodded and took Karin's hand. She didn't let go until they'd walked through the exit on the other side of the park.

'I haven't seen you in thirteen years,' Karin's mother said to Daichi. 'I thought you lived in America.'

'I've been living in New York for a long time, but I'm relocating back to Tokyo. Now that I'm going to be living near here, I'd like to spend some time with my daughter. . .' Daichi said as he turned and gave Karin's mother a warm smile, '. . . and I'd like to spend some time with you as well if you're okay with that?'

'Of course,' said Karin's mother. Her voice was now kind and caring and Karin smiled to herself. She was so pleased to see the softer side come out in her mother. It was a side she was very used to seeing but she knew her mother rarely let her guard down for anyone else and maybe with her father back in their lives it would bring back some of the happiness that had eluded her mother for so many years.

Karin had lunch with her mother and father for the first time ever at a Soba restaurant near the park. Now that Karin knew the strange man was actually her father she looked at him in a completely different light as they all slurped their Soba noodles. Karin tried to covertly study her father's face in between mouthfuls of her buckwheat noodles but every time he glanced at her she would quickly return her gaze to the bamboo basket cradling the cold noodles in front of her, as if she was totally absorbed in her meal. She would then wait until her parents were engaged in another lengthy conversation before looking again at her father's face. Karin noticed they shared the same big eyes and full lips and she liked the fact she'd inherited the high bridge on her nose from her father as well. When she wasn't studying her father's face she was listening intently to the tone of her father's voice and she decided he was a very amicable person and they would definitely be great friends in the future.

Karin listened to her mother and father talk together as though they'd never been apart. As the hour progressed, Karin's back straightened with pride, feeling for the first time she was part of a proper family and Karin enjoyed every moment of just being able to sit with both of her parents at the same time.

Karin was curious about how her father was able to recognise her when he hadn't seen her since she was two years old. 'How did you know it was me when you saw me in the park?' she asked him.

'You saw Karin-chan in the park?' Karin's mother blurted out. She looked shocked that Daichi had tried to approach her daughter prior to their reunion that day.

Her father coughed uncomfortably as if his daughter had asked a question he would rather leave unanswered.

'Now please don't get angry,' Daichi said to Karin's mother who looked suspicious, but not upset when Daichi pleaded with her. 'Your grandmother sent me a photo of Karin-chan on her twelfth birthday with a short letter begging me to contact both of you. Your grandmother was so kind – she told me you were a very good mother and a hard-working woman and Karin-chan had a very sweet and generous personality.'

Her mother's features softened when Daichi mentioned Karin's grandmother and out of respect for her own deceased mother, Karin knew there was no way her mother could get upset about the fact Karin's grandmother had sent a letter to Daichi without her knowledge.

Daichi asked Karin about how she was coping after her grandmother's funeral but when Karin looked down at her hands and he could see how upset she was about losing her grandmother, he sensed this was a sensitive topic and he quickly switched to asking her questions about how well she was doing at school. When he mentioned her friend Mai, who he'd obviously seen with her on several occasions, he told Karin he thought Mai looked like a true and wonderful friend. Karin's mother and father laughed when Karin told them she couldn't believe she and Mai had run away from her own father.

As Karin ate her meal slowly, hoping to drag out the meal as long as possible, she could see her mother was holding back any old grudges she'd had for the father of her only child and Karin hoped that now her father was back in Tokyo on a permanent basis, they could spend more time together. Karin thought to herself with warmth and comfort in her soul that her father didn't look like the person she'd always imagined him to be, but he certainly had the heart of a man who wanted to make up for lost time. Karin made a promise to herself she would always be the daughter he'd never had, now and forever, and even if they never lived together in the future as she'd so often hoped for when she was much younger, at least they could all be good friends.

Homeless in Shinjuku

Mariko was twenty-five years old, five feet tall and she had a slim build. Often people, especially family and friends told her she was very pretty and charming but Mariko was not a vain woman and when she looked in the mirror every morning, as she applied her makeup and brushed her hair, she saw just a regular face and figure and a person with an average personality.

Twelve months before, Mariko had married a lovely man called Katashi and she thought she'd done very well for herself, securing a husband who she personally rated as being better than above average in many ways and someone who could help her to secure everything she wished for in life. They'd been friends for many years and she'd always known he was the one. It comforted her to know he'd always felt the same way about her. She definitely considered herself to be a very lucky girl. Mariko and her husband Katashi didn't have any children but they talked about how they'd like one girl and one boy in the future. Katashi worked in Marunouchi for a large and very well-known fishing company and Mariko work in Shinjuku for a much lesser-known but respectable IT company as a secretary.

Every week day, Mariko would drape herself in fine wool gabardine suits and pure cotton work shirts and every morning she'd step out in her expensive Italian heels as she made her way to the exciting and stimulating business district of Tokyo with her husband Katashi by her side. Mariko thought they looked like a very happy couple with a promising future as they sat together side by side on the train, checking their smartphones and smiling at each other's messages.

In the evenings, Mariko would wait for her husband at one of her three favourite coffee shops for an hour or two until she'd meet with Katashi in front of the west exit at Shinjuku Station for the commute back to their compact yet comfortable house just outside Tokyo.

Both Mariko and Katashi loved working in the business districts of Tokyo. They thrived on the adrenalin of the rush hour pedestrian traffic and they held their chins up high and smiled smugly at the modernity, power and authoritarian wealth which surrounded their places of work. They felt at one with the sea of suits that would swell in and out of the surrounding platforms of the many subway stations. Mariko and Katashi both loved to collect the latest gadgets, gizmos and technologies that complemented their lifestyles and they enjoyed all the creature comforts their salaries could afford them. They were always looking to improve their already high standard of living.

One chilly Thursday evening in March, Mariko received a message from Katashi telling her he wouldn't be able to meet her until eight thirty p.m. and Mariko decided she'd walk a different way through the subway under Shinjuku Station in search of a new coffee shop where she could sit and watch the passers-by as she waited for her husband. There was still a large throng of people about, returning home from their places of work or making their way to the many eateries in the area, craving a quick and cheap meal like yakitori, katsu curry, udon and soba noodles, conveyor belt sushi or just a bottomless jug of beer. Others dressed in more expensive suits were searching in groups for restaurants where they could enjoy teriyaki, teppanyaki and the more expensive kaiseki dining. Mariko was far from alone as she weaved her way through the underground lanes towards the café/restaurant/cheap boutique area. She was not fully alert because it had been a long day at the office and she was looking forward to a caramel flavoured coffee, topped with whipped cream and chocolate shavings. Mariko knew she'd be eating out later at a restaurant with Katashi but she felt like she needed some sustenance if she was going to have to wait until eight thirty p.m. for their supper.

The scent of warm bread from a pop-up bakery made Mariko hesitate and consider buying a small bun to stave off the grumbling in the pit of her stomach. As she was looking at the delicious morsels on offer at the bakery, Mariko heard a man calling out her name. She turned around to see who had cried out to her. The voice was charming and quite gentle and it sounded like the person knew her.

'Mariko-chan, is that you?' asked a man who she did not know. 'I can't believe it's you! Don't you recognise me?'

Mariko stopped dead in her tracks out of fright and her cheeks flared up with embarrassment. The man who had called out my name was not someone who she recognised at first and certainly not someone to whom she'd normally speak. It was obvious to her and she knew it would be clear to everyone surrounding her that this strange person in front of her who was calling out for her attention was homeless and Mariko was immediately humiliated that someone as well dressed and as proper as herself would have to communicate with someone so grubby, dishevelled and repulsive. Mariko's first thought was to ignore this bizarre creature but he did have a kind smile and a familiar face which made her hesitate and she was slightly intrigued that he knew her name. The homeless man stepped gingerly towards her. The shock that Mariko felt inside did not provide her with the ability to move or to talk at first. What she did notice was that several amused people were watching the homeless man edging his way towards her and they were just as perplexed and as astonished as her.

'How do you know my name?' Mariko finally asked the homeless man who was dressed in a crumpled and stained dark blue suit.

'I'm Ryōichi,' he said to her. 'I'm your brother-in-law. Don't you remember me?'

Mariko knew that several strangers who were waiting in line at the pop-up bakery were watching and listening to this peculiar conversation and even though this seemed like one of the most embarrassing moments of her life, the realisation that this homeless man was actually her brother-in-law and considering the fact she knew he'd always had a kind and sympathetic personality, Mariko set aside any prejudice she'd felt up until this point and she stepped closer to Ryōichi so as to bridge the gap between them. It was difficult at first to find the right words and Mariko felt like she was swaying a little as if Ryōichi's breath had pushed her head and her shoulders back from her body, as she tried to adjust to this situation which she'd never have predicted. It had been eight years since she'd seen her husband's brother and both Mariko and her husband hadn't spoken about Ryōichi for a long time. Mariko remembered her husband had told her Ryōichi had gone off the rails when he'd been about thirty-five years old. First, he'd lost his job and having no wife or family to support, he'd gradually allowed the cracks to form in both his professional and private life. Her husband had told her many years ago that Ryōichi had started sleeping all day and he'd adopted such an indifference to normality that it wasn't long before he could no longer pay his rent of ¥120,000 per month or sustain any way of looking after himself properly. Katashi and Mariko had stopped receiving calls from Ryōichi for quite some time and he had not visited them at their home for many years.

Mariko and her husband Katashi had been friends since childhood. They'd started dating from about the age of seventeen and the two of them had been so caught up with the enjoyment of their own lives that they'd just accepted this was Ryōichi's path in life and it wasn't long before they'd forgotten all about him, although his exclusion from their lives had never been carried out with any form of malice.

It took Mariko a few seconds to recollect her thoughts but somehow she managed to pull herself together and force out some kind of reply.

'Nice to um . . . um . . . see you again Ryōichi-san,' Mariko said. For the next few seconds, she took the time to reassess her surroundings and she quickly realised Ryōichi was not really a threat, albeit this meeting was somewhat humiliating for her.

Ryōichi was standing in front of what appeared to be his home. This was a cardboard box draped in blue nylon sheeting. The box would have been large enough for two people to sit down inside it at a squeeze. Surrounding Ryōichi's makeshift home were six other similar boxes, which on closer inspection were all carefully constructed and personalised to comfort and protect the other people who chose to live as homeless transients in the subway below Shinjuku Station.

'How is my younger brother?' asked Ryōichi.

'Fine,' Mariko replied with the nicest smile she could muster, not very willing to share their lives with Ryōichi or to continue any type of friendly conversation even though he was part of the family.

Ryōichi took another step closer towards Mariko and this time she took a step back away from him with a new shock. It startled her to see the future of her husband's face mapped out on Ryōichi's face in front of her. Ryōichi's grey hair and lined features represented what her husband's face might look like fifteen years on and after the initial shock it was difficult for her not to feel a strong connection between herself and Ryōichi. Mariko wanted to do something to help her husband's brother and her first thought was to reach for her purse. Mariko rummaged around in her handbag to find some money for him. She hoped that by giving ¥1,000 to Ryōichi, she was doing the right thing. She'd also begun to feel the eyes of the people around her again and she wanted to be able to wrap up this conversation and flee to a coffee shop where she'd be able to escape back into the comfort of a world that she could deal with more easily. She desperately felt the need to get back to her familiar surroundings like one of her favourite coffee shops, instead of being in this very awkward predicament. As Mariko opened her purse and pulled out a crisp and clean ¥1,000 note, shame swept over Ryōichi's face and Mariko instantly felt terrible for thinking of giving him money and treating him like a charity case. It was troubling for her to watch him stare down with a look of intense hurt at his old shoes which were full of holes.

Ryōichi slowly raised his head and looked up at Mariko. 'I can't accept your money,' he said. 'But I'd like a cigarette. Do you have one?'

'I'm sorry, I don't smoke,' Mariko replied as she quickly squeezed the money back into the pocket of her purse.

'Are you okay, Ryōichi-san? Are you happy?' Mariko asked him as she leaned forward and tried to be nice, ignoring the strangers who glared at them, knowing she'd definitely offended Ryōichi with her offer of cash but she didn't want to continue to seem unfriendly towards her husband's brother.

'Yes . . . I'm very happy,' Ryōichi replied.

The sincerity in his eyes told Mariko he was being honest. Ryōichi may have smelt like stale cigarettes and he would have known his home was worth nothing but his forehead told a story of calmness and acceptance.

'Are these people your friends?' Mariko asked him, indicating towards the other makeshift homes around them where several other homeless men were lounging at the entrances to their cardboard caves.

'No, but I do have friends,' Ryōichi replied. 'I have the pigeons that I feed in the park and I used to have a stray cat which I called Kitty but I haven't seen her for about a week. I think she'll come back soon.'

'Oh,' Mariko said, not really knowing what to say to someone in his position and feeling pity for her brother-in-law who only considered stray pets as friends. 'Do you receive any government benefits?'

'No,' Ryōichi replied. 'I refuse to wait for hours to talk with anyone in their administration. Their cold glares and their indifference is more than I can bear . . . anyway I don't have a fixed address and I'm not ill so I can't receive benefits because of this . . . I'm just happy and at one with nature . . . sometimes I get money for garbage that can be recycled and I also do some cleaning for the Metropolitan Government buildings.'

From where Mariko was standing she could peer into his cardboard home. She noticed it was very neat and clean. There was even a makeshift kitchen and a kettle inside and a rope stretching from one side to another to dry out Ryōichi's clothes. On the floor Mariko saw a futon and a couple of blankets tucked neatly underneath. Four instant noodle cups were lined up on a temporary shelf and some bread that had probably been donated by the surrounding shops was wrapped in a plastic bag near the kettle.

'I have to go,' Mariko said to Ryōichi, afraid he might invite her into his cardboard home.

'Are you going to meet my younger brother?' Ryōichi asked her.

'Yes,' Mariko replied with a warm smile.

'Please tell him I wish him all the very best,' he said. 'It was very nice to see you again Mariko-chan.'

'Thank you,' she replied. Mariko waved at Ryōichi as she headed back away from Shinjuku Station and walked toward a FamilyMart convenience store which she'd seen earlier that evening.

Ten minutes later, Mariko handed Ryōichi a packet of twenty Seven Stars' cigarettes. She felt a feeling inside her she hadn't felt for years when he bowed several times and seemed so grateful she'd bought him something he'd really wanted. It was the warm and fuzzy feeling a person gets when they've been truly and sincerely considerate of others. Ryōichi's thankful face and the enthusiasm in his appreciation would stay in Mariko's memory for many weeks to come.

An hour later, Mariko met her husband Katashi in front of a coffee shop in Shinjuku Station. He was very pleased to see her after a busy day at work. Mariko waited until they'd reached a nearby restaurant and they'd sat down and ordered their yakitori before she told Katashi about her encounter with his brother Ryōichi. Mariko was delighted when Katashi asked a lot of questions about Ryōichi's health and his predicament and she agreed with him when he announced that he wanted to do whatever he could to help him. Together, Mariko and Katashi decided to gather together a box of gifts that would include a couple of warm blankets, some green tea, some snacks and a carton of cigarettes and they made plans to return the following week to present these to Ryōichi.

Unfortunately, the following Wednesday at seven p.m. when Mariko led Katashi to the exact spot where she remembered meeting with his brother Ryōichi in front of the pop-up bakery, Ryōichi was nowhere to be seen and Mariko couldn't locate his cardboard hut with the blue nylon sheeting anywhere. Katashi suggested they ask one of the other homeless men about Ryōichi's whereabouts but after the first homeless man they approached gave them a blank glare and scuttled away laughing, they decided their efforts were futile and they had to give up.

For the next few weeks, Mariko wandered around Shinjuku Subway Station looking for her brother-in-law but she didn't have any luck finding him. She could only conclude that the weather was becoming warmer and Ryōichi had relocated to an entirely different area. Mariko often thought about Ryōichi as she sat waiting for her husband in a coffee shop every evening after work, hoping she'd see him again one day. Mariko did take comfort in the fact she'd met up with him after so many years and he'd looked happy enough living his alternative lifestyle. Mariko liked to think about the fact, as she sat sipping her caramel lattes and waiting for her husband's phone call to tell her he'd finished work, that her brother-in-law had shown her how important it was to count her blessings and to never take for granted everything that money could never buy.

Retail Reality

Monday was certainly an eventful day at work. Our manager Keiko announced at the weekly staff meeting that Junko, our assistant manager, was leaving permanently to live in Hokkaido. Although I was sad to see her go, the really interesting news was that her position would be replaced internally and that gave us all the chance of promotion.

I'd been selling clothes full-time at this store in Futako-Tamagawa for over six years. Michiko, sitting to my right, had been the only other full-timer for the past five years. The three casual members on our team, Akiko and Yasuyo sitting to my left and Naomi sitting to Michiko's right, were all final year university students and all three of them lived at home with their parents. These three all had much grander future prospects in mind and wouldn't be interested in a career in retail. I knew Michiko would be my only rival for this dream job.

I glanced at Michiko, trying to read her body language. She was definitely interested in the position. As she turned to me and smiled smugly, the fire in her eyes told me she was ready to fight for the job. I glared back at her and held her gaze. The game was now on. I sensed it would be a fierce competition. Only one of us could become the new assistant manager and as far as I was concerned, the position was mine.

Admittedly, I'd become quite disillusioned with my work over the last three years. I thought back to when I'd first started several years ago. I remembered looking forward to the introduction of each new line of garments at the start of each season and I'd even enjoyed every stocktake. I used to always take the time to think about how to coordinate one piece with another from the current season, even when I wasn't working. I'd arrive thirty minutes before we opened to prepare myself for the day and I'd greet each and every customer with an impressive bow as they entered the store with my usual vigour and conscientious professionalism. I'd also set myself personal sales targets each hour, hoping my manager Keiko would put in a good word for me at head office and fast track me into management. Years ago, I would have really loved the opportunity to head either the Shibuya or the Daikanyama boutiques but as each season passed, my dedication and my dreams also faded away.

After years of trying to be the best of the best in retail I realised my career was going nowhere quickly and I gave up constantly trying to impress my manager. I'd begun taking extended lunch breaks to reduce the number of hours I'd have to spend on the sales floor and I'd arrive late for work two or three times a week. I'd lean on the shop counter and check messages on my mobile phone when Keiko was on a break and I'd hide in the stockroom and make phone calls to my boyfriend Hachirou, while pretending to reorganise stock. Michiko would do the same and we'd always cover for each other if Keiko started questioning our efficiency.

The staff meeting finished and we threw on our coats, scarves, hats and gloves. Naomi unlocked the door to the shop to let us out and we huddled outside in the freezing cold waiting for Keiko to pull down the security shutters and lock up for the night.

'So Junko is leaving,' said Michiko. 'Who do you think they'll choose to replace her Reiko-chan?' she asked me. The evil grin on her face told me she thought she was the perfect person for the job.

'Well, I've been here the longest, so that would be me,' I replied.

'But my sales have been much better than yours for the last three months and Keiko told me I'm management material!' Michiko teased.

'You're lying,' I blurted out, 'Keiko never said that to you.' I hoped I was right and Keiko had never actually said this to Michiko.

'Okay, that's true, I'm lying but you know I'd really like to be an assistant manager,' Michiko continued.

'And so would I,' I yelled back as I walked away. I'd already started dreaming about allocating all the daily tasks to the other girls while I took it easy in the back office and I could see myself buying a new outfit every month with the extra money I'd earn.

I walked past the Takashimaya Department Store, it was still open and I decided to have a peak at their latest line of women's fashion before heading home. As I wandered around looking at the luxurious labels on offer, I admired the quality of the faux fur on the collars of the gorgeous cashmere coats and I stroked the soft, buttery leather on the imported Italian boots. It didn't take long for the sales assistants to realise I had no money to spend and most of them didn't bother me as I wandered around dreaming of wearing such expensive brands. I knew I was dressed well and my look was coordinated in the latest designs from the new winter range that our shop would sell over the next few months, but anyone could see my clothes had neither the finish nor the expense that was displayed all around me as I wandered through Takashimaya.

Feeling despondent, I skulked out of the department store and headed for the bakery. I'd have to live on steamed rice sprinkled with Japanese condiments or cheap bread from Le Boulanger Dominique Saibron for the next two weeks if I wanted to get a new pair of boots I had my eye on. After buying two black olive and sundried tomato focaccias as well as an escargot sweet bread for just ¥799, it was time to return home to my small apartment in Sangenjaya. I walked slowly to the train station trying to think of the best strategy to claim the assistant manager position. Keiko had said in the meeting that Miss Aya, our area manager, would be visiting the shop in the morning. Maybe I'd pull her aside and have a word.

I woke up an hour earlier than usual the following morning, planning to be better organised and wanting to look my best. I washed my hair, curled it to perfection and ironed my cream blouse and silk scarf. After dressing and applying my makeup, I carefully folded my futon into three and pushed it into the cupboard along with my blanket, duvet and pillow before slipping into my six-inch heels at the door. As I left the house, I was feeling confident walking towards the station. Although my hair needed a trim and the collar on my jacket was pilling, I was quite sure I'd impress Keiko and the area manager that day.

My boyfriend Hachirou and I had plans to go out for dinner later that evening in Shibuya. He worked part-time at the Tipness gym located next to Loft, a specialist lifestyle store, not far from Shibuya Station and we would always meet outside Loft every Tuesday. From here we would rush to a restaurant of his choice. He once told me he always liked to spend the last couple of hours of his day thinking only about what he was going to eat for dinner that evening and this didn't surprise me at all. Hachirou clearly exerted himself at work and whenever he worked out. His rippled chest and his toned shoulders were a fine example of his disciplined exercise regime and he never put on weight or looked flabby despite the fact he liked to eat fine food when we met in Shibuya at six p.m. every Tuesday. Whenever I met him in front of Loft he was always pulling his face in a way that reminded me of a starved puppy because he was so hungry. He would get angry with me if I arrived late for our dinner date and I always felt guilty if he had to wait longer than ten minutes for me. If Keiko asked me to clean up the shop at the last minute or if the till wouldn't balance and I had to work out why, I'd sometimes have to take the later train from Futako-Tamagawa Station and run from Shibuya Station to meet Hachirou, knowing he was always on time and waiting impatiently for me. I'd find him outside the Loft store walking up and down in one spot, sometimes holding his stomach and rolling his eyes at me as he greeted me with exasperation. Hachirou would spend the next five minutes telling me off for keeping him waiting for so long when I was well aware of how much he enjoyed his food after a long day and a strenuous workout session.

I knew Hachirou hated to eat alone and deep down I also knew that in his mind I was probably just a female body who was happy to sit with him in a restaurant as company and I was easily replaceable if I ever dared to complain. Hachirou didn't like to eat at the many cheap ramen, yakitori or burger bars scattered throughout Shibuya. He'd always insist on eating at proper restaurants. Hachirou would often remind me he had a sensitive stomach and he couldn't eat just anywhere. A few months earlier, he'd explained to me on the way to a top-end yakiniku restaurant that he'd once had food poisoning from a street stall yatai and ever since that night he only liked to eat at a restaurant which had a proper menu and a waitress to bring him his food. Hachirou's family was very rich and they still gave him pocket money even though he was twenty-five years old. Unlike me he always had a lot of spare cash which meant he could eat out, shop as much as he wanted and he didn't have to work full-time. He only worked a few hours every week as a gym instructor where he'd spend his time pushing weights and maintaining his gorgeous physique.

I often wondered how many other girls sat and watched him eat the expensive meals he enjoyed so much and whether they felt as insignificant as I always did next to Hachirou. I knew I would never be the one to capture his heart as I watched him sitting opposite me every Tuesday, realising he was much more interested in the plate in front of him than the new dress I was wearing that night or the fact that I'd taken a lot of trouble to curl my hair in a certain way just for our date. We'd often spend a whole hour eating together without sharing a single word. I'd twist my hair and admire Hachirou's fine bone structure in silence as he ravenously devoured his sirloin steak or as he managed to eat his portion and most of my portion of a sukiyaki or shabu-shabu hotpot. Hachirou was the best looking boy I'd ever dated and I often considered myself lucky to spend time with him and I did appreciate the fact he always insisted on paying for our dinners. We'd met through friends and I knew that although I was just one of many girls he liked to date, I had to accept the fact that it was nice just to be seen with someone so muscular, fit and good-looking. Occasionally, I would be in two minds about whether I was actually going to meet up with Hachirou for dinner. It worried me that my relationship with him was just as dead end as my job in retail but I hadn't met any other boy who was happy to take me out, who was as good-looking as Hachirou and who was this generous to pay for all these expensive dinners. At the end of the day, I'd make up my mind to keep seeing Hachirou until a true love stepped into my life. Hachirou was never going to date me exclusively but it was difficult not to admire him for his looks and the way his shoulders rippled when he'd take off his jacket or how kissable his lips were when he pouted them in frustration when I arrived a few minutes late for our date.

When I arrived at the shop forty-five minutes early on Tuesday, I was still thinking about Hachirou and our date that night as I began counting the float at the till. I greeted Akiko and Keiko when they arrived not long afterwards with a big smile but my positive attitude went out the window when I saw Michiko walk through the door, dressed to impress. Her hair had been blow dried and she was sporting professional looking curls tied back with a Salvatore Ferragamo tortoise shell clip. Not only this, her eyes were big and bright thanks to perfect makeup and a set of thick and fluttering false eyelashes.

'Thank you for making an effort. You look terrific Michiko,' said Keiko. 'I wish all my staff members would go to so much trouble when the area manager is coming in.'

Michiko looked very pleased with herself. Deflated, I decided to spend some time in the stockroom, telling myself repeatedly not to let this get me down.

The area manager, Miss Aya, arrived when I was out at lunch and I returned to find her deep in conversation with Michiko in the back office. I waited my turn out front in the shop, spending longer than usual trying to assist potential customers but I'd failed to make even one sale when Miss Aya emerged. I'd never get my chance to have a meeting with our area manager that afternoon. Miss Aya came out telling Keiko she had to rush off to the Daikanyama store for a meeting and she wouldn't have time to chat with the rest of us that day. I wasn't too worried about this as I'd spent a full hour working with Miss Aya the previous month and I knew she'd been really impressed by my sales techniques.

Miss Aya turned to me just before she left. 'Keep up the good work Reiko-chan,' she cried out to me, flashing me a super smile, as she walked out of the store. That boosted my confidence up a notch. Michiko looked at me positively seething. Maybe her meeting with Miss Aya didn't go quite as well as she'd hoped, I thought to myself. It was still game on.

On Tuesday afternoon Keiko informed us that we'd all find out about the new assistant manager on Friday. She looked straight at me when she told us this news and I was almost certain I was going to be chosen to do the job.

That night, I spent another uneventful date with Hachirou. I tried to start a conversation with him about how excited I was about the assistant manager position on the way to a new Italian restaurant his friend at work had recommended, but we were walking so fast I completely gave up on the idea of talking about myself. When I nearly twisted my ankle as I half-skipped and half-hobbled along behind Hachirou in my six-inch heels, zigzagging our way through the Shibuya streets in our haste to get to the Italian restaurant and have dinner as quickly as possible, I decided it was impossible to have a normal conversation at this pace.

As we sat eating in a fancy Italian trattoria forty-five minutes later, I tried to enjoy my spaghetti marinara but I was disappointed my only real conversation with Hachirou was about how much he would have preferred the waitress to grate fresh parmesan cheese straight onto his chicken cacciatore with tagliatelle rather than having to serve himself from a bowl of grated parmesan which was already on the table when we arrived.

The next couple of days were a flurry of hard work, commitment and dedication. Michiko made a ¥35,000 sale on Wednesday afternoon but I went one better than her and sold a jacket, a pair of trousers, shoes and a handbag worth ¥55,000 on Thursday morning to a rich lady who came into the store with her young daughter, wearing matching coats. It turned out they were travelling to Europe and they were doing a big shop in the area, and I was more than happy to help them out and impress the manager with my sales.

* * *

The alarm clock didn't need to wake me on Friday morning. I was up and out of my futon an hour early. I sang in the shower and danced into a flattering wool dress which I'd bought in the sales twelve months ago. Coat, scarf and hat on, I rushed to the shop with a skip in my step.

I was fumbling with my keys as I approached the store, preparing to open the security shutters, when I noticed a lone customer waiting for the store to open. She was wearing an expensive looking teal funnel neck coat from our new winter range. Her hair was tied back in a chignon and she looked friendly and happy that someone had come to open the shop.

'I'm sorry but we don't open for another half hour,' I said, crouching down to turn the key in the lock.

'I'm not a customer. I'm your new assistant manager,' she replied. 'My name is Nana.'

I couldn't believe it. Exasperated, I let go of the key and the shutter snapped up hitting the top of the door with a bang. 'I didn't mean to do that,' I said apologetically, looking up to see if I'd broken the security gate.

'You should be more careful with that,' Nana said, shaking her head and rolling her eyes at the same time.

Great, I thought to myself, she's already telling me off and the day hasn't even begun.

Michiko arrived ten minutes later and I took her to one side and told her about Nana. We stood side by side, arms folded, both of us deciding she wasn't old enough to tell us what to do. After discussing Nana's negative and positive attributes for several minutes, Michiko gave me a determined nod and strode straight up to our new assistant manager and asked her the question on everyone's lips.

'So Nana-san, how did you get the assistant manager position?' she asked.

'I used to work full time at the Daikanyama store but I took time off to complete a course in retail management,' replied Nana. 'I phoned Miss Aya to tell her I was ready to come back to work and she offered me the position at this store in Futako-Tamagawa.'

Michiko and I went to the back office and talked about the merits of doing a course in management but we both decided it wasn't for us.

Over the next eight hours work returned to normal. Sales figures went back down and Michiko and I both came back late from lunch. I covered for Michiko when she went out for a sly cigarette and Michiko told Nana I was in the bathroom when I snuck out to meet Hachirou for fifteen minutes behind the shop. He'd just bought a new car and he wanted to show off the big red shiny beast of a vehicle in the car park behind the store. I oohed and ahhed and told him I couldn't wait to go for a ride in his new Subaru Impreza and we agreed he'd pick me up on Sunday and take me out to a French restaurant in Harajuku. Hachirou looked so sexy in his fur-trimmed jacket and his faded Levis and when he blew me a kiss as he drove away I realised our short conversation had centred entirely around him and I didn't get the chance to talk to him about my frustrating dream of becoming the next assistant manager and how my hopes of becoming a manager at this store in Futako-Tamagawa had just been dashed.

I spent the next couple of hours trying to look busy, dusting the shelves and refolding all the shirts. I decided to adopt a different attitude and I thought I'd tell my family and friends I'd never really wanted to become an assistant manager and the shop where I worked now in Futako-Tamagawa was not busy enough for me to have ever seriously considered a management position.

It was very clear to me that my job and my boyfriend were not making me happy. In fact, I thought both situations had become endlessly tedious and boring and I decided later that night I'd go on the internet and look for a more exciting retail position. I'd always enjoyed going out in Ginza and I knew this was a place that was always filled with fabulous shops and people. I spent the rest of my day at work dreaming about working as a manager for a famous fashion company like Prada or Gucci. I also pictured myself not too far into the future walking through Matsuya Department Store in Ginza with a man not quite as good-looking as Hachirou but someone a lot nicer who adored spending time with me and who would lavish me with gifts and love, lots and lots of love.

Perfection

Naoko and Fumie were sisters but their personalities were worlds apart. Naoko liked knitting, attending ikebana classes or learning to play the three-stringed shamisen. She spent her evenings reading the *Asahi Shimbun* newspaper and watching wildlife documentaries on NHK television. Fumie preferred to go out on the weekends and practise her bad English conversation skills on the young American marines who frequented the nightclubs in Roppongi. She'd also spend her weekends shopping for the latest designer clothes in Aoyama or painting her nails in intense, glossy shades from her favourite nail varnish brand Chanel, and sometimes she'd treat herself to a decadent facial or a holistic massage at a luxury establishment in Tokyo, like the Peninsula Hotel in Yurakucho.

Naoko on the other hand did everything she could to maintain a peaceful lifestyle. She always woke up with the birds, she'd prepare for herself a well-balanced Japanese breakfast of grilled fish, steamed rice and miso soup and she'd tidy up their apartment and feed her two goldfish before heading off to work. There she'd spend eight hours at her predictable and repetitive job, typing all day as a data entry processor for the Sumitomo Mitsui Banking Corporation in Maranouchi.

Fumie would get up at about noon, skip breakfast, spend an hour deciding what to wear, take another thirty minutes to apply her make-up and leave their apartment at around two p.m. to work a three hour shift at the SK-II cosmetic counter inside Takashimaya Department Store in Ginza.

Despite their differences, both Naoko and Fumie had been living together for just under three years since they'd moved out of their parents' home in Saitama. It was their mother who'd begged Naoko to move in with Fumie, asking her to watch over her youngest daughter. Their mother had hoped Naoko as the older sister would be able to keep Fumie on the straight and narrow. At first, Naoko had been hesitant and reluctant to live away from the family home with Fumie but after just a few months living together in Setagaya, Naoko had realised the opposite sides of their personalities allowed for the perfect living arrangement. Fumie encouraged Naoko to take it easy and her older sister motivated Fumie to get out of bed in the morning and think about earning a living. Fumie would often go out with her girlfriends or on a late night date with a variety of different good-looking but pretentious young men. She'd often creep into their apartment between five and six a.m., make-up smeared and hair in a tangle, trying not to wake up her sister so as to avoid an argument later in the day about where she'd been all night. Little did she know Naoko didn't mind that her sister spent so much time out of the apartment, as this provided for her the peace and quiet she'd always favoured.

Fumie was twenty-six years old and two years younger than Naoko. She wore her extremely long hair in a variety of styles all the time. Sometimes her long locks were curled, at other times wavy and once in a while she wore it straight. It was always dyed a different colour depending on her mood at the time. At the moment, it was jet black with a burgundy rinse running through it. A month beforehand, she'd opted for a blue-black rinse. Naoko on the other hand, had a conservative shoulder-length hair style that was easy to manage. It dried in no time after a wash and she only had to run a comb through it for a second before she went out. Naoko liked everything in her life to be manageable and stress free.

Naoko was quick to notice as the years passed by and as Fumie grew another year older so did Fumie's desires to perfect the way she looked. At twenty-six years old, Fumie now wore more make-up than she'd ever done before. Naoko was relieved her sister worked for a make-up counter which meant she could buy all her expensive skin care products and cosmetics at cost price and Naoko knew this must have helped save Fumie a fortune. The only other cosmetic products Naoko saw in the bathroom cabinet that were not from SK-II, were the Chanel nail varnishes and as they were a lot less expensive than the full range of SK-II face moisturisers and elixirs that were neatly stacked next to the nail polishes, this did not worry Naoko in the slightest. Her younger sister had waxed off her eyebrows six months earlier and she'd had them tattooed on instead which gave Fumie a more polished and less natural look. Naoko's eyebrows were much bushier and often in need of plucking and occasionally she'd let Fumie attack them with the tweezers, but Naoko never enjoyed the experience. She'd only give in to her sister after constant nagging.

Fumie would also spend up to ninety minutes, three times a week, running counter-clockwise around the five kilometre Tokyo Imperial Palace Loop in Chiyoda ward in central Tokyo with thousands of other joggers, but only when the weather was fine as she didn't like to get her long hair wet when it rained. Later she'd head to the gym to tone up with weights and use the tanning machines to maintain her fake tan which gave Fumie a healthy-looking glow. Fumie had become obsessed with working on each individual muscle group in her body at the gym and she was very careful not to develop any flabbiness, especially under her upper arms and around the thigh area. The most frustrating part of Fumie's obsession to look perfect was when she was going out somewhere with Naoko. She'd make her sister wait for hours, taking painstaking care to get ready, while Naoko sat waiting for her, gradually getting more and more frustrated in the living room.

It didn't surprise Naoko at all when Fumie came home from her job at Takashimaya one evening and announced she'd made an appointment with a plastic surgeon at the private hospital near their home to discuss the possibility of rhinoplasty. Fumie made Naoko look at her nose from every angle while she explained how the shape of her nose could be improved. Naoko responded as she usually did when she thought her sister was completely over-reacting, by telling her there was absolutely nothing wrong with her looks, but this time Naoko could tell Fumie was determined to undergo the procedure. Naoko had seen this look in her sister's eyes before and she knew Fumie's mind had passed beyond all normal reasoning and there was no way to stop her doing whatever she planned to do.

'I've seen different ladies walking in and out of that private hospital for years and they always look so happy and confident,' Fumie said to Naoko who had given up objecting and was now holding her head in her hands in exasperation.

Naoko had also noticed the clients coming in and out of this fancy institution. It was a modern white building with pristine, almost sterile looking lines and bubble-shaped windows which reflected the fact that this was no ordinary public hospital and it only dealt with the wealthiest clientele.

'A customer at work today was talking with me when she came in to buy a moisturiser and she suggested I contact Dr. Hayashi who works at that hospital – he was the very doctor who worked on her own nose and it was such a pretty nose Naoko-chan,' said Fumie. Her head was bobbing about in excitement and her eyes were wide. 'Obviously I was very discreet but I managed to ask her a lot of questions about her nose and when she left my counter a rhinoplasty operation was all I could think about all afternoon and so I've already made an appointment with Dr. Hayashi at the clinic.'

Naoko could imagine Fumie spending the whole afternoon at work looking in the mirror on her counter studying her nose from different angles instead of serving prospective customers.

'Did you sell a lot of skincare products today?' Naoko asked her sister, knowing the answer before Fumie had a chance to respond.

'How could I?' replied Fumie. 'I was too busy thinking about the perfect shape for my new nose!'

Fumie knew that Naoko had the following day off from work and she pleaded with Naoko to accompany her to the appointment she'd made for the next day with the plastic surgeon.

It was ten a.m., only fourteen hours after Fumie had convinced Naoko to go with her to her first meeting with Dr. Hayashi. They both left their apartment building and walked five minutes down the road and into the private hospital. After slipping through the automatic sliding glass doors at the entrance they were greeted by a young receptionist with chiselled features and perfectly straight bleached white teeth. They were asked to take a seat in the waiting room for their ten fifteen a.m. appointment.

Naoko noticed two other ladies, both of them very well-dressed, one in a silk navy blouse and fine wool trousers and the other in a cashmere beige wool dress clutching a Prada handbag, sitting side by side completely at ease in the reception area. They were both flicking through fashion magazines waiting to be called into the inner sanctum for their consultations. Naoko also noticed they showed no signs of nervousness and she thought to herself that this was not the first time either of them had been there for various nips or tucks.

Fumie was dressed just as nicely as the other two women. She'd spent over an hour the evening before deciding whether she should wear her caramel-coloured suede leather jacket or a new cream coat that she'd just recently purchased from the latest Max Mara collection. Fumie had finally decided to wear the suede jacket and she was happily fidgeting and flicking through magazines, occasionally pointing out to Naoko what she thought were perfect noses on the faces of strikingly beautiful fashion models, while they waited to see the doctor.

The lady in the navy blouse had looked up briefly when Naoko and Fumie had entered the waiting room. She'd looked straight past Fumie at Naoko with a raise of her eyebrows and Naoko translated the look as one of complete disbelief that Naoko had chosen not to dress up like they had done to come to such an exclusive private clinic. Naoko knew straight away that her black Uniglo trousers and her pale pink sweater which she'd purchased four years earlier seemed very out of place in these elegant surroundings but she wasn't really bothered. Instead Naoko took pride in her modest appearance, reminding herself that her healthy bank balance was a reflection of her thriftiness.

At ten twelve a.m., a nurse called out Fumie's name at the door of the waiting room and the two sisters followed her down a hallway covered with modern art and into a plush office where Dr. Hayashi was expecting them. He was sitting in a well-padded leather armchair with large brass studs impressed into the edges. The receptionist offered Fumie and Naoko a cup of tea or coffee which they both declined before she left them to sit down in this beautifully furnished room with impressive wood panelling lining the walls.

After a very formal initial greeting and a low bow to the ladies, Dr. Hayashi who looked a lot younger than they'd expected sat down again as slowly as he could into his chair as though he was suffering from a bout of arthritis and he could only move very carefully or he'd be subjected to considerable aches and pains. Dr. Hayashi launched into a discussion about the particulars of rhinoplasty surgery. He asked Fumie about her medical history and he also explained the side effects of anaesthesia, the potential complications of nose surgery and he was keen to let them know about the extent of his experience. He spent a further fifteen minutes discussing with Fumie the benefits of a chin implant if her new nose looked out of place with her new facial features. The last ten minutes was spent looking at computer imagery to find the perfect shape for Fumie's new nose. Naoko was a mere spectator and all she could do was sit back and watch Dr. Hayashi charm Fumie until her sister was completely brimming with enthusiasm.

There was an interesting feature on Dr. Hayashi's left jaw line that Naoko could not help but glance at over and over again. It was a deep pinkish scar that ran across his chin and up the outside of his left cheek. She thought it was interesting because instead of detracting from Dr. Hayashi's good looks, it actually improved his desirability and added to his masculinity. Naoko also noticed how Dr. Hayashi's eyes looked over Fumie's face unlike any other man she'd seen stare at her sister's striking good looks. It was as if he was drawing lines on her face and deciding which other areas could do with some surgery to improve her appearance. Naoko thought Dr. Hayashi might very well be calculating the profit he could make from more surgery, as he silently counted out each conceivable procedure. In turn, Naoko stared at different parts of the doctor's face, although her eyes could not help returning to his deep scar. She tried to see if the doctor had undergone any cosmetic surgery himself to improve his looks but she couldn't see any tell-tale signs of this at all. Naoko was attracted to his strong nose, his large, bright brown eyes and the flicker of grey hair above his ears. At the end of the meeting Naoko was disappointed to leave, having enjoyed watching Dr. Hayashi's remarkable and unique features and listening to his calm and controlled voice as he explained all the aspects of each procedure.

Fumie left the private clinic with Naoko, completely convinced that rhinoplasty was a surgery she really needed and it was something she should have had done years before. As they walked back through the corridor towards the reception to the glass sliding doors, Fumie chatted happily to her sister without expecting a reply, excited to proceed with the plastic surgery, but Naoko wasn't listening. She was a bit disturbed by the greetings from the three nurses who passed them at different times on their way out. It seemed to Naoko like they all had the same straight bob hair style, and even more strangely exactly the same smile and demeanour. This left Naoko with an eerie feeling that would haunt her thoughts and her dreams for the next few weeks.

Fumie planned to have the surgery exactly a fortnight later and she spent every waking moment discussing the procedure optimistically with anyone who'd listen. Naoko imagined her describing her new nose with every woman who stopped at her SK-II make-up counter and with all the other girls who worked in the cosmetic hall at the Takashimaya Department Store in Ginza. Naoko was subjected to even lengthier discussions after Fumie returned from each of the three extra consultations she had with Dr. Hayashi when they'd look at the preoperative photography and they'd discuss the shape of her new nose. Fumie had also bought a couple of fashion magazines every three days before the operation and she'd cut out different pictures of the models with noses which she really liked so she could ask Naoko and Dr. Hayashi which ones they liked the most and which ones would suit her the best.

Naoko and Fumie had both been left a considerable amount of money from their grandfather when he'd passed away four years earlier, which meant the sisters were never short of cash. Naoko sometimes wished they'd never received this, which would have meant Fumie would have been forced to be much more considerate about how she'd spend her money.

Over the next couple of weeks without knowing why, the consultation at the private hospital had an unexpected and bizarre effect on Naoko. She was plagued by strange nightmares night after night, after their meeting with Dr. Hayashi. In some of these disturbing dreams, she could see different images of his long scar coming at her and reaching out to scratch her own face, until she was left horribly mutilated. In another nightmare, the scar would turn into a mouth and warn her to be careful, while different nurses with the same bob haircut and the same ghoulish smiles would wander in and shake their heads from side to side as they faded in and out.

As each day passed and the day for Fumie's surgery approached, Naoko began to feel more and more edgy about whether her sister had made the right decision to have an operation on her nose and even more procedures in the future, but when she tried to discuss this with Fumie her sister would laugh at her and tell her to stop acting like a cynical and conservative old woman. During the last few days before the operation, Naoko urged Fumie to at least check out the testimonials from Dr. Hayashi's former patients but her sister kept telling her she was being overly cautious and she'd never expected her to approve of what she was doing.

On the day of the surgery, Naoko promised Fumie she would collect her from the recovery room and she tried to be really positive and optimistic when she watched her younger sister getting ready to leave the apartment building. That morning, Fumie even looked a bit fearful and nervous about the decision to have the operation which was going to completely change her looks.

As promised, Naoko left work early at two p.m. so she could help her sister to get home in the afternoon. As she left the train station closest to their apartment building, she stopped at a convenience store to buy a newspaper and some ready-made sushi for her to eat at home before heading down to the hospital to pick up Fumie.

Fifteen minutes later, Naoko dropped down and slid under the kotatsu coffee table in the living room at her home and opened up the packet of sushi so she could spend a quiet half hour enjoying her lunch and reading about current affairs in the newspaper before she had to collect her sister from the hospital. Naoko squeezed out the soy sauce and the wasabi from their small takeaway packets and snapped her disposable chop sticks before slowly relishing each piece of salmon and tuna sushi which served as a very satisfying lunch. She was a bit tired and she didn't have the energy to read every single article in the *Asahi Shimbun* newspaper. She just read the headlines to pass the time. Naoko finished the last piece of sushi and she leaned forward on the table to hold the newspaper with both hands as her eyes scanned the black and white pages. "Young Boy Saved from Drowning in River", "Prime Minister Promises a Better Future" and "Cold Weather until Tuesday", were

some of the headlines that caught her eye, but she stopped and pushed the newspaper away from her in horror when she read "Scarred Plastic Surgeon Deforms Patients' Faces". Naoko's mind felt like marshmallow and small, dark spots appeared before her eyes, as she threw the empty sushi packaging and the chopsticks into the clear plastic bag in which she'd bought them. As she tied the bag she jumped up in a panic and looked around for her handbag.

Naoko kept telling herself that she knew there had been something strange about Dr. Hayashi and the nurses who worked at the private hospital where her sister was now being operated on and all she could think about was how quickly she could get to her sister before the scarred doctor deformed her sister's pretty face.

A multitude of negative possibilities were running through Naoko's mind as she ran out of the door of her apartment and speedily made her way to the private clinic. She kept thinking about how they should never have trusted Dr. Hayashi and how her mother would blame her if Fumie's pretty face was destroyed for life. She wished now that she herself had looked into the doctor's background and how negligent she'd been when it had come to her sister's welfare.

It only took a few minutes for Naoko to reach the hospital. As she skidded to a stop at the glass doors, Naoko smoothed down her hair which had been swept to one side from the windy weather outside and patted down her skirt which had ridden up to her hips when she'd been running. There was no receptionist at the desk and as Naoko walked past the entrance she didn't see anyone in the waiting room either. Determined to find Fumie, she walked down the hall and past the consultation rooms towards the back of the clinic where the operations took place. A minute later she found a door marked as the recovery room and she took a deep breath before pushing it open with the sweaty palm of her left hand. Naoko was not surprised there was nobody around but she was really hoping and praying that Fumie would be lying inside the recovery room ready to greet her. There were three beds inside lined up with the pillows facing the door but they were all empty. Naoko noticed a couple of bandages speckled with fresh blood stains on the bedside table to the side of the bed on the far right and something inside her told her Fumie had been there but she had now been taken away. Naoko kept telling herself she was too late as she dropped to the foot of the last bed on the right. She held her head in her hands with tears in her eyes as she fought to think clearly and tried to decide what to do next but all she could think about was Dr. Hayashi's deep scar and the nurses' strange smiles.

Naoko heard the door to the room creak open behind her and she turned around wearily not knowing what to expect. Fumie and a nurse stood looking down at her with concern.

'Naoko-chan, what are you doing on the floor? Are you all right? Why are you crying?' asked Fumie.

Naoko quickly sprang back up and shook herself, realising she'd jumped to a lot of conclusions and she hadn't really thought the matter through, as she quickly tried to come up with a reasonable excuse for being in the recovery room. 'I felt faint and I was looking for someone to help me but I'm okay now.' Naoko said as she smiled awkwardly at the nurse and peered up at her sister, whose face was wrapped in bandages, knowing they must have thought she looked very peculiar sobbing on the floor in an empty room a long way from the front reception where she should have been. 'Are you okay Fumie-chan? Did the operation go well?' she asked her sister.

Fumie replied that the operation had been very successful and she was feeling fine.

The nurse who had probably seen more unusual situations than the two sisters combined, nodded at Fumie and Naoko and took charge of the situation. 'The operation went very well. Your sister Fumie-san was an excellent patient,' she said. The nurse walked to the left of Naoko and guided the two sisters out of the room and down the hall. 'Would either of you like a warm drink before you leave? It's very cold outside.'

'No thank you,' replied Fumie, 'I'd rather go straight home but I really appreciate everything you've done for me. I'll come back soon for my follow-up consultation with Dr. Hayashi. I'm sure my nose will look great. You've all been very nice. Thank you again. Goodbye. Well, let's go Naoko-chan.'

Later that night after Naoko had tucked Fumie into bed and promised to check on her in the morning, she opened up the *Asahi Shimbun* newspaper to read the article about the scarred doctor who had deformed his patients. Naoko discovered that this doctor worked in India and had absolutely nothing to do with the private hospital located down the road in Setagaya. The constant nightmares that had recently pervaded so many of her dreams had left her very weary and hypersensitive during the day. Naoko was usually very practical and well-grounded and she felt embarrassed for mistrusting such a reputable clinic that had taken such good care of her sister.

Over the next few weeks, Fumie's bandages were gradually removed to reveal a much more streamlined nose that suited her features immensely. Naoko's nightmares disappeared in correlation with Fumie's satisfaction and although Naoko resisted every attempt from her sister to have a little bit of work done on her own face, Naoko had to agree with Fumie that Dr. Hayashi had done a marvellous job improving her sister's face.

* * *

Three months later, Fumie arrived home after three hours of work at the cosmetic counter at Takashimaya, declaring to her sister that she'd like to get blepharoplasty. Fumie explained to Naoko that this was a double eyelid surgery to reshape the skin around her eyes to create an upper eyelid with a crease which would make her eyes look more like those on the faces of the Western girls she'd seen in her favourite fashion magazines. Naoko just rolled her eyes and agreed with her, thinking at the same time she'd better take a few photographs of her sister now before Fumie became too obsessed with plastic surgery. She looked anxiously at her sister's face which was evolving before her very eyes, thanks to the rhinoplasty and clever makeup techniques. Fumie's face was already very different from the one she'd known when they were children. It was with genuine concern that Naoko wanted to take photos of Fumie before her sister made even more adjustments to her appearance, in her elusive quest to maintain a youthful appearance and in her aim for what her younger sister liked to call absolute perfection.

Bully Boys in Yokohama

Shoji was Hansuke's new best friend. In fact he was Hansuke's only friend in Tokyo. In December, Hansuke and his family had moved from Kyoto to Yokohama for his father's new job. They'd been in Tokyo for about six weeks.

Hansuke was only fourteen years old and in the third term of his second year at the local public junior high school which was situated not far from where he now lived with his family in their new home. In fact, it was only about forty minutes away. The school didn't have the best reputation and Hansuke learnt very quickly that the teachers never really showed much interest in their students.

Hansuke and Shoji's friendship was formed in the first week at his new school. Shoji was the only person who'd been nice enough to sit next to him in the cafeteria on his third day there. No-one else had made the effort to get to know him and for the first few days Hansuke truly thought he was being deliberately ignored by the other students in his classes and he wasn't wrong, but he counted himself lucky they didn't him hassle him. Shoji was different – he was quiet and unassuming and interested in the same manga and anime that Hansuke liked to read and watch.

Hansuke had left three close friends at his school in Kyoto but it didn't take him long to realise he wasn't very popular in Yokohama. Hansuke had never wanted to leave Kyoto. He knew it always took him a long time to make friends because he was fairly quiet and he was missing his hometown and the buddies who he'd known for years and who he'd left behind in Kyoto, a city he'd always love. Even at a young age, Hansuke had felt a profound appreciation for the fact Kyoto, the city where he was born, was so beautifully preserved and a lovely place to live. His home had been close to many Buddhist temples, Shinto shrines, Zen gardens and the Kyoto Imperial Palace. Yokohama, in contrast, was a busy, bustling place and Japan's second largest city with a population of over three million people. Life was faster in the Tokyo area and it seemed a lot more complicated compared to his hometown Kyoto, a place renowned for its serenity and beauty.

Within just a few minutes, Shoji and Hansuke bonded very quickly as they sat eating their lunch together and chatting quietly. Hansuke was really pleased with himself; he'd made a new friend in just a few days after starting at his new school. He was quite a self-conscious young boy and he didn't like the idea of having to sit all alone during the forty minute lunchtime period.

Hansuke was taller than Shoji but they were both relatively thin and puny at fourteen years old. Shoji had just become the same age as Hansuke after his birthday four weeks before. Neither Shoji nor Hansuke were very good at any kind of social interaction but they instantly became good friends, recognising in each other that they both felt awkward and uncomfortable around most people. Neither of them had any brothers or sisters and they'd both spent a great deal of time by themselves growing up in homes where they'd had to create their own fun while their parents concentrated on making a living and working hard. When Hansuke and Shoji first met, they realised neither of them had any siblings. This made them both feel like they shared a common bond and they were equally special and unique.

Hansuke liked Shoji from the moment they first met and he knew they would be great buddies, but he soon became aware of a very difficult situation at this new school which explained why Shoji was looking for someone to be his friend. Hansuke liked hanging out with Shoji and for some reason that he could not explain he felt like an older brother to him. He sensed that Shoji really needed his support, but it took him a few days to realise Shoji was caught up in the middle of a bad set-up at the school. Shoji didn't know how he could explain this to Hansuke and although he was waiting for the right time to tell him, it wouldn't take long before he would find out what was going on and Hansuke would also became part of the problem.

On Tuesday in the second week at his new school, Hansuke was sitting with his friend Shoji in the cafeteria. They were quietly eating their lunch and chatting about the comic book Shoji had bought the day before, when a large, spotty faced boy who Hansuke had never seen before came over and flipped over both their lunches onto the floor for no apparent reason. Hansuke turned around to see two of this belligerent boy's friends pointing and laughing at them as Hansuke bent down in shock to clean up the mess. Within seconds, Shoji took hold of Hansuke's sleeve and dragged him out of the lunch room, not letting go of him until they reached the playground outside. Both boys leant against a tree puffing and shaking and Shoji began to explain why they'd both had their lunch knocked to the floor. He told Hansuke he'd been having trouble for the past few months with the same group of three fifteen-year-old boys who were a year ahead of them at school. He apologised to Hansuke for choosing him as a friend when Hansuke knew nothing about how he was being bullied on a regular basis. Hansuke, not aware of just how much his friend was being tormented, immediately vowed to stand by him but Hansuke would soon realise that this decision may have been a big mistake.

Over the next few weeks, Hansuke and Shoji were humiliated almost every day by the pimple faced boy and his friends. The two young and vulnerable boys were usually intimidated by these bullies during their lunch break, when they were poked with flick knives and forced to hand over their bento lunch boxes.

The three bullies were called Masashi, Akira and Ikuo. Masashi with the spotty complexion was the ringleader and the meanest of the three. He was tall and willowy and always snarled and glared at anyone who walked past him. Akira and Ikuo were the punks who backed him up. They were wrestling champions and enjoyed throwing their weight around. These three boys talked about the tattoos they were planning on getting and how they liked to hang out in the red light district known as Kabukichō in Shinjuku, as well as what they wanted to steal from the local shops. They'd been picking on Shoji for over twelve months before Hansuke met them and they'd decided to turn their sadistic attention on Hansuke as well, when they saw him sitting with Shoji in the cafeteria.

Two weeks later, Hansuke found out again just how frightening Masashi, Akira and Ikuo could be when they approached him and Shoji in the schoolyard after a game of baseball and told them they were the bats and Hansuke and Shoji should accept that they were the baseballs and they needed to keep hitting them so they could continue their "game". Masashi and his friends mocked Hansuke and Shoji as they pushed them with the ends of their bats, forcing them to turn around in a small circle over and over again until the two boys were so dizzy and disorientated they fell to the ground. As Hansuke watched the bullies run away laughing, he looked down at Shoji who was fighting back tears and he couldn't stand the idea of abandoning his new friend to these merciless thugs.

Hansuke had noticed that some of the boys and girls in his class had walked past them in the playground when these nasty boys were poking them with their baseball bats and he'd seen them giggling as they watched Masashi and his friends taunting them. Hansuke realised the other students were well aware that if these three boys were picking on Shoji and Hansuke then they would be left alone and their own need to protect themselves outweighed any desire to help him and Shoji. This meant Shoji and Hansuke would never have a wider group of friends to support them.

The following week, Masashi, Akira and Ikuo waited for Shoji and Hansuke as they were leaving school at the end of the day and as they were heading out of the school gate. Akira and Ikuo stole their wallets before Masashi told them he'd cut them up with his flick knife if they didn't shoplift sweets for them from the convenience store opposite the school. Luckily the cashiers never noticed the boys stealing anything, but both Shoji and Hansuke were left shaking and very nervous even though they'd managed to get the sweets and hand them over to the bullies. To make matters worse, they'd returned home without the wallets the three brutes had promised to return to them.

Hansuke wondered whether Masashi and his small gang would ever show them any mercy and he hated the way they enjoyed hitting, kicking, ridiculing and alienating Shoji and Hansuke as often as they could. Hansuke found out Masashi was originally from Osaka and he himself had been teased when he first arrived at this junior high school and although Hansuke often thought about this, he couldn't understand why Masashi constantly told him off for using the kansai dialect. Every day the bullying seemed to get worse and Shoji and Hansuke started having trouble coping with their school work and concentrating on their studies.

Hansuke began thinking about how he could get Shoji and himself out of this situation as he laid in bed every night, unable to sleep. Hansuke finally decided that the best idea would be to stay away from the school and it didn't take him long to convince Shoji that this is what they should do. Shoji and Hansuke talked about playing truant for four days before they had the courage to start doing it. They were both too scared to walk through the hallways or to stop at their lockers when the teachers weren't around and they would keep away from the schoolyard where the bullies could easily find them during breaks, as they discussed their plan to permanently get away from these nasty boys. They'd chatted about the possibility of talking about the situation with their home room teacher who also acted as a counsellor but they'd decided she probably wouldn't do anything. Shoji and Hansuke had also discussed mentioning the problem to their parents, but they both knew that their parents had enough problems of their own, working long hours at their jobs, and they didn't want to cause them any more worry. When Ikuo told them that only last year there had been a student who'd complained about bullying and he'd been expelled because the teacher had denied any probability of it happening, Shoji and Hansuke decided they couldn't put up with this any longer and that was the last day they showed up for any of their classes. They decided to return after the school term had finished and Masashi, Akira and Ikuo had moved on to the senior school.

Shoji had a vulnerable and considerate side to him and because he was painfully shy he'd nearly always agree with everything Hansuke suggested. He didn't even question Hansuke's idea that they should stop going to school. Hansuke had really grown to like his new friend Shoji in this short amount of time and he was looking forward to enjoying their time together away from the bullies. Truancy seemed like the perfect option.

Shoji and Hansuke decided to spend their days at Hansuke's house in his bedroom, where they could play video games, read comics and watch television every day when they should have been in classes. They came up with a plan which allowed them to do this without their parents' knowledge. Hansuke's father had begun work as the newly appointed manager at the central post office in Yokohama and his mother had taken on a full-time position as a nurse in the local hospital. His parents were both hard workers and they'd often comment on how important it was to show dedication to your chosen occupation.

Shoji's parents were also extremely diligent workers. They owned their own cake shop and they spent long hours there in the shopping mall outside the SOGO department store in downtown Yokohama.

Both parents were so busy working that neither of them noticed Shoji's nor Hansuke's absenteeism from school and after about three weeks Hansuke and Shoji realised their plan had worked as they settled into a much happier life, safe in Hansuke's bedroom, playing games, eating snacks and sometimes trying to do some school work when they felt guilty about not going to their junior high school.

Hansuke knew his parents would never suspect he was playing truant if he was careful. He'd always been the kind of boy to follow the rules, do his homework and get a good report card. His mother was a very kind-hearted woman and his father was a proud man who was extremely dedicated to his work. He'd often tell Hansuke that he should be proud of his father now that he was a manager at the post office and it was the kind of job they only gave to honest and respectable citizens. Hansuke's parents had never had cause for concern about their son in their past and they'd hardly ever had reason to reprimand him when he was younger. If Hansuke did speak out of line or didn't finish all of his dinner, his mother would ruffle the top of his head as she told him off and Hansuke's father would always buy him presents to compensate for his angry tone if he ever spoke harshly to him.

Hansuke realised Shoji's parents would probably never find out they were playing truant because he was such a quiet boy but Shoji still needed to be more careful with his parents as they liked to ask him questions about his day. Shoji panicked at the beginning of the truancy when he told Hansuke his mother nearly always asked him about his studies when she came home from work. Hansuke told him that the best way to respond to this was just to say it had been a good day and to keep his reply as short as possible, making sure he had his head buried in a textbook whenever his mother asked him about his school life.

Hansuke knew his mother was always tired when she walked in the door and she had trouble communicating with Shoji because she knew he was very quiet, so she'd never hover at Hansuke's bedroom door for too long. Also when she arrived home from work Shoji would often have already left to return home to his own house. Hansuke also knew his mother would be thinking about the fact his father would be home soon and she would be worrying that she didn't have a lot of time to prepare the dinner.

Every morning, Hansuke gave his parents the impression he was still going to school. When his alarm woke him at seven a.m. he'd immediately get up, take a quick shower, put on his black trousers and his military-style junior high school blazer with its standing collar over a white shirt that his mother always ironed for him the night before. After this, he'd sit at the table to eat a piece of toast or a croissant with his parents. Just before leaving home, he'd throw a pile of textbooks and a few notebooks into his schoolbag which he'd carry downstairs before picking up his bento box and saying goodbye to his parents as he put on his loafers at the entrance to their home. At the start of his truancy he would stare at his mother's face for a minute before leaving to check for any suspicion in her eyes but he knew he didn't have to bother about doing that anymore. His parents never showed any sign they suspected he was doing anything he shouldn't. His mother and father were too busy cleaning up the breakfast table and preparing for work to notice anything unusual. Hansuke knew his mother and father left the house together to go to their respective work places at least thirty minutes and at the most forty minutes after he walked out the door. Hansuke would always walk in the opposite direction to his parents towards the FamilyMart convenience store which was located about twenty minutes down the road.

Up until a few weeks ago, when the two boys were still attending school, Shoji and Hansuke would always meet at the FamilyMart convenience store to walk the last twenty minutes to their junior high school but now they'd buy snacks and drinks instead and head back to Hansuke's house. By the time Shoji had met Hansuke and they'd finished paying for their refreshments and walked all the way back to Hansuke's house, his parents were long gone. Luckily, Hansuke's home was surrounded by tall bushy red pine trees. They could walk all the way up the drive and get into the house without the neighbours noticing what they were doing.

The boys used to worry about missing their classes and at the beginning of the truancy they would study conscientiously for about two hours between ten a.m. and twelve p.m. every morning. They'd agreed between themselves that if they watched an NHK documentary on television every now and then and if they did two hours study every day, they'd have studied enough to be at the same level as the other students. They decided that if they were behind on their Japanese language lessons they'd make up the time to learn more kanji characters and read textbooks on Japanese grammar and they convinced themselves that nobody would know they'd missed school. Even though Hansuke and Shoji tried to be as conscientious as they could, gradually the time they dedicated to their school work was reduced by ten minutes every day and finally they gave up opening their textbooks altogether. They just nibbled on their snacks, drank sodas, read comic books, watched cartoons or played Final Fantasy on Hansuke's Xbox.

Hansuke and Shoji were both naturally neat people and they always cleaned up after themselves. They wouldn't have wanted anyone to think they'd acted slovenly during their truancy. They were good boys deep down and in the first couple of weeks both of them felt a little guilty about not going to school, but after a while they didn't care too much about this and they just enjoyed spending all their time doing whatever they pleased.

After a few weeks, even staying at home and playing all day started to bore Hansuke and Shoji and they began talking about the fact that they should return to junior high school the following term in April. They discussed how they'd be able to convince their parents they'd graduated from their second year of junior high school and they could see themselves just slipping into their third year a few months later without anyone noticing.

It had been three weeks on Friday since Shoji and Hansuke had started playing truant and now all the bullying they'd had to endure had become a distant memory for them. Hansuke never seemed like a sensitive person to Shoji but he'd never told him how he used to come home and cry into his pillow after the bullies had ridiculed him. Hansuke knew he had to be strong in front of his friend and he knew Shoji relied on him to make the decisions to ensure they were both safe.

They'd been studying alongside forty other students in their classes at the junior high school in Yokohama and Shoji and Hansuke had come to the conclusion that they weren't even missed when no one raised the alarm that they were absent. There were a lot of students packed into each of the classrooms and Hansuke quickly realised when he began at the school a few weeks earlier that there were too many students in each class for him to receive the individual attention from the teachers which he'd received when he'd attended the junior high school in Kyoto. Hansuke told Shoji that this could be the reason why they were not missed at all.

Towards the end of his truancy, Hansuke missed the opportunity to join in the activities arranged by the after-school clubs and he knew that Shoji was a little wizard in mathematics and he missed being the first in the class to solve difficult formulas but neither of them mentioned the possibility of ever returning to school before the first term started in the first week in April.

* * *

Three months later, Hansuke and Shoji returned to their junior high school in Yokohama to start the first term of their third year after a long truancy. Masashi, Akira and Ikuo were nowhere to be seen – they'd all started their first year at a senior high school which was over ten miles away. The teachers and their fellow students never said anything about the fact the two boys had been absent for so many weeks.

Hansuke and Shoji approached their studies with a renewed energy and enthusiasm to do well. During their breaks and at lunchtime they would play happily outside but occasionally when they heard a few of the other boys shout out, both Hansuke and Shoji would turn around in fear only to laugh nervously together when they realised they were not being targeted and humiliated and there was no longer a chance of them being bullied. Tears would well up in their eyes as they looked at each other anxiously and resumed whichever game they'd been playing. Although they didn't say anything, every time this happened they both couldn't help thinking about Masashi and his nasty friends and they were relieved these horrid boys had moved on to the senior school and they were now safe.

A Startling English Lesson

Matthew had been full of high hopes when he'd begun his teaching career. He used to jump out of bed at six a.m. every morning with a smile on his face and drive to the local high school singing along to the radio. He used to greet the other teachers in the staff room with enthusiasm and take great care preparing his lessons for the day. He'd been certain he was going to make a big difference to the lives of these young pupils who nowadays ignored him and sat half-asleep and indifferent, waiting for the bell for the class to finish. The young boys and girls who he'd wanted to inspire had ended up draining Matthew of any motivation and now he was just someone who the students looked straight through and most often ignored. When they did take any notice of Matthew, he was treated like the inane subject of a documentary who these adolescents were forced to watch over and over, like the replay of a boring video rather than a real human being with a purpose and an agenda. He'd been teaching at this same high school in Essex for three years and he'd had enough.

Matthew was in his late-twenties and he liked to look respectable. He kept his thick, curly black hair short. He never left his studio flat in Chelmsford, the county town of Essex in the East of England, without shaving.

He showed up every day to work in one of his three reasonably expensive and well-fitting navy suits, which he'd bought all at once on sale from a well-known shop called Austin Reed on the High Street, but he was well aware he now lacked the right attitude for his academic career and for just about everything in his life in general. He'd had no dates with any girls for six months, he had nothing to say these days to the other teachers at work, he owned no property, his friends were all getting married and they were completely satisfied with their lives and as well as this he was becoming increasingly embarrassed driving around in his battered, silver Volkswagen Golf Hatchback. It had been perfect ten years earlier when his parents had bought it for him second-hand, but this previously much loved vehicle was now leaking oil, the paintwork was beginning to rust and it was making very peculiar sounds whenever he started the motor.

Matthew felt it was time for him to do something different, it was hard to know what would help him but something told him that it would need to be a radical change. He needed to rekindle the passion he'd once had for his life and his job, he needed to find a new direction.

It was one Monday evening in July, after Matthew had spent the whole weekend lying on the couch at his parent's house being chastised by his mother for moping around, unable to talk about how exasperated he was with his current predicament, when he began thinking about how cool it would be to work in another country. After several Google searches, Matthew found a blog about a young woman who was teaching English in Osaka. Matthew knew very little about this city in Japan but he'd always wanted to go to Tokyo and see a place he'd read about called Akihabara, which was famous for its electronics and technology. Matthew spent another couple of hours searching for potential teaching jobs in Tokyo and he finally came across the perfect job vacancy at a private English school in a town called Roppongi. Matthew read the details of the position three times and as each minute passed so did his sense of dread about his future. For the next four hours, Matthew surfed the internet to find out everything he could about living and working in Japan. He'd always thought you needed to speak Japanese to work in Tokyo but when he did more research he realised no Japanese language skills were necessary. His excitement increased when he found out he could earn double his current salary and work fewer hours if he moved to the other side of the world where everything was different and a lot more exciting than everything he'd known about his working life up to that point in his career.

Ten weeks later, Matthew had travelled to Japan and he was happily living with eight young Australians and Americans in shared accommodation in Roppongi, a district of Tokyo which was full of foreigners. Matthew only had to work four days a week and he often spent his nights drinking, dancing and partying with his new found friends in and around Roppongi in bars and nightclubs, which were all in walking distance of his accommodation. He'd also spend a few hours every weekend wandering through neon-lit Akihabara, marvelling at the latest electronics and technology. His favourite store was Yodobashi Camera located on the east side of Akihabara Station. Whether it was the latest in computers, home audio, cameras, smartphones, watches or even hi-tech home appliances such as digital rice cookers and robotic vacuums, everything fascinated Matthew and he felt like he'd stepped into the future.

Matthew's attitude towards life was now very different. He had loads of energy, he loved the way his students commented on what a great English teacher he was, he enjoyed meeting a bunch of new people; he couldn't get enough of the tasty and healthy Japanese food on offer, and he had every intention of staying in Japan for a long time, making a lot of money and celebrating life to the full. He was very aware of the fact he'd come straight from a job where he'd taught a group of young people who no longer had any respect for the education system in Essex. Tokyo was a place for him where Japanese adults willingly paid a lot of money to improve their English and simultaneously they always showed him a huge amount of respect as they admired his teaching methods.

Matthew enjoyed six months of teaching, as well as eating out, dating various girls from all over the world, a few evenings singing karaoke and lots of drunken nights in Roppongi and Shibuya. He really liked his new carefree and happy-go-lucky lifestyle but one Monday after work he realised that if he took on some more private English teaching positions he could increase his weekly wage by forty per cent. He knew other teachers who were earning double his salary from private English tutoring to individuals and Matthew started to get money hungry. That Monday afternoon, he scanned *The Japan Times* newspaper for possible English teaching jobs but there were no private positions advertised and he could see that a lot of the work wouldn't fit in with his current working schedule.

He decided to head to the local shop and buy some milk for his tea and to get some fresh air to clear his head. Fifteen minutes later, he was just about to enter the local supermarket, where he usually bought his daily groceries, when he saw a friendly-looking advertisement in the store's window which was highlighted with pink smiley faces around the headline "English Tutor Wanted". It said that a lady called Rika was looking for an English teacher and she was prepared to pay the princely sum of ¥5,000 per hour for private English lessons at her home in Nishi-Azabu, not far from Roppongi. Matthew asked the shop assistant, who he'd spoken with several times in the past and who he knew was quite fluent in English, how long the advertisement had been in the window and when he replied that it had only been up for an hour, Matthew removed the sign carefully and slipped it into his back pocket.

Matthew rushed back to his shared accommodation to call the number on the advertisement, not realising until he was almost back to his room that he'd forgotten to buy the milk that he'd intended to buy from the shop in the first place. He decided he'd get his groceries later as he quickly greeted a couple of Americans at the entrance to his home for foreigners and bolted to his room to make a phone call. Inside he wasted no time dialling Rika's phone number. A woman with a fairly deep voice, who sounded a lot older than him, answered the phone and when she realised Matthew was not Japanese she happily spoke to him in quite good but broken English. Rika explained her husband was a diplomat and they would be moving to London in eighteen months and she wanted to speak better English. She was thrilled Matthew was from England and she told him she had lots of questions for him about living in the United Kingdom.

After speaking with Matthew for just a few minutes Rika told him she already thought he would be the perfect English tutor for her. Rika wanted Matthew to teach her English four hours per week, two hours on Friday and two on Sunday and she said she'd be happy to pay ¥20,000 per week in total. Matthew couldn't believe his luck as he rubbed his hands together and made a quick calculation in his head, realising he would be earning nearly ¥70,000 a week from all his jobs if Rika was pleased with their English conversation classes. Matthew was more than happy to agree to meet with Rika the following Friday when she explained the easiest way to get to her home in Nishi-Azabu would be if they met outside Hiroo train station at two p.m. When Rika asked Matthew how she'd recognise him, he replied that he was six feet two inches tall, he had short black curly hair with blue eyes and he would be wearing faded light blue jeans and a grey sweater. He told Rika he would be difficult to miss if she saw him standing outside the station on Friday because he was so tall.

Just as he'd promised, Matthew exited Hiroo Station on Friday at exactly two p.m. wondering what Rika looked like and expecting her to be in her late forties or mid-fifties and probably old fashioned but kind and sweet looking. He was presuming all this based on her gravelly voice, her maturity and her slightly strange-sounding conservative way of speaking English. It was with some surprise, at two minutes after two p.m. that Matthew turned around to see a very petite but elegant woman in her late twenties, about the same age as him, dressed in cream ankle boots, a flattering indigo coloured pair of blue jeans and a soft brown leather jacket with a wide shearling wool collar. Rika called out his name as she crossed the street and approached him with a very welcoming smile. Matthew watched Rika's smile widen even more as his mouth dropped open in unexpected surprise. He could hardly find the right words to say as Rika introduced herself and they began walking away from the station along a tree lined street.

'It's beautiful day,' said Rika.

'Yes, it's *a* very beautiful day,' said Matthew.

'Ah yes, the indefinite article, I need to learn to use the indefinite article properly,' Rika said.

'Wow, your English is very good if you already know about the indefinite and definite article,' said Mathew enthusiastically. Matthew loved teaching English, especially to people who enjoyed being taught.

'My apartment is over there,' said Rika, pointing towards a very fancy and modern apartment building further down the street.

'That's very convenient,' replied Matthew with a smile, impressed by how nice Rika's building looked.

Five minutes later, Rika and Matthew entered through glass sliding doors and walked past a young male concierge who greeted them with a nod but no expression as he sat at a formidable light oak reception desk in a burgundy suit and navy tie. Matthew found his voice again as they took a mirrored elevator up to the fourteenth floor and he realised these English conversation lessons were a dream come true. He explained to Rika that he was living in Roppongi and he also commented on how much he loved Japan.

Matthew was really looking forward to teaching someone so beautiful looking in a lovely apartment for a lot of money. Rika opened the door to a large apartment, apologising for the mess, which was basically a random cushion that had fallen off a large, floral and comfy looking sofa onto the floor of a very plush open plan and stylishly renovated home. Matthew was pleased to see they would be conducting their English conversation lessons at a long maple wood dining table surrounded by ten plush light blue velvet high back formal chairs, rather than on a low table on the floor. His long legs meant he could never get used to the Japanese custom of sitting on the floor for long periods.

Matthew had brought along with him one of the English conversation books that he used at his regular four day a week job to help him get through the two hour conversation lesson. He decided he'd start halfway through the textbook because of Rika's advanced English level. He was preparing the lesson in his head as Rika made them both a cup of Earl Grey tea and he was ready to start when she brought over two cups of black tea each with a thin slice of lemon swimming on top, as well as two pieces of strawberry shortcake on plates.

'Your home is lovely,' said Matthew, as he took the cake and the white fine bone china cup and saucer from Rika and carefully placed it on the table to his right.

'It's very simple,' replied Rika, waving away his flattery.

'Are you kidding?' said Matthew, 'This apartment complex is really luxurious and I've never been in such a large apartment in Tokyo. You have granite worktops in your kitchen, gorgeous light fittings and your furniture is grander than anything I've ever owned. It's really nice. You must love living here.'

'It's okay. I'd prefer to live in a house,' said Rika.

Matthew instantly picked up on the fact Rika was just being modest, like many other Japanese people who he'd met over the last few months and he could see by the flushed grin on her face that she was well aware her home was lovely and she was equally flattered by his compliments.

'You also have a wonderful view from your window,' said Matthew, having just noticed how pretty the tree-lined street looked beyond the balcony outside the living room. He thought to himself that Rika's husband must have a very well-paid job for them to live in such luxurious surroundings. The size of the apartment was as large as the accommodation for foreigners where he lived which housed eight people.

Matthew took a sip from his tea, hoping he wouldn't spill any and ruin the polish on such an expensive dining table. He realised he'd better start the lesson and leave the cake until later, knowing that if he wasn't professional enough he might lose out on this golden opportunity to earn ¥20,000 a week from Rika. He also wanted to tell her she was very pretty but he was intelligent enough not to mention this to a married woman while sitting alone with her in such a nice apartment and he certainly didn't want to make her feel uncomfortable.

Matthew adopted the professional face he'd always used when he used to teach his young students in England and he began the lesson, deciding to talk about food and restaurants. They'd been discussing the correct way to order from a menu for just a few minutes when, for the first time since Matthew had been in Japan, the table began to rattle and both Rika and Matthew said the word "earthquake" in English at the same time. Rika reached for her fine bone china plate and cup and saucer and Matthew picked up his as well, knowing that if he didn't grab them they might chip and he could see they would be very expensive to replace. He'd heard about earthquakes in Japan but he'd never experienced one before and he thought to himself that if it was just a little commotion like he was feeling now then he would have nothing to worry about. Just as Matthew began to offer some reassurance to Rika, the whole room started to sway back and forth like a boat on choppy waters and Matthew's smile as well as his confidence disappeared.

'What should we do?' he asked Rika who could see the fright in his eyes instantly.

Matthew really had no idea how to cope, never having been in this situation before and never expecting an earthquake could be this scary. It was like nature had taken a grip on his throat and it was starting to apply pressure. He was a little bit reassured by Rika's lack of panic as the side to side motion of the whole apartment switched to more of a shaking up and down and his teeth began to chatter along with the movement of the whole room.

'We need to get under the table,' Rika replied.

'Wouldn't it be better to get out of the building?' said Matthew, ready to run to the door. 'Or at least go out on the balcony.'

'No, we're on the fourteenth floor. The elevator will not work and it would be dangerous to be out on the balcony,' said Rika. 'The safest place is under the table . . . please trust me Matthew-san.'

Matthew and Rika pulled their chairs back and as they awkwardly clung on to their teacups and plates, they knelt down and dived under the maple wood dining table. As he did so, Matthew spilt the tea and his lemon slice onto the beige deep pile carpet but Rika quickly picked them up and didn't seem at all concerned about the stain. Thirty seconds later the room started to sway again from left to right and Matthew became even more alarmed. He'd never known anything to be as powerful as this and he wished he wasn't on the fourteenth floor.

'Hold onto the legs of the table to steady yourself,' said Rika.

'I don't want to steady myself. I want to get out of the building. I have to go, I'll take the stairs,' said Mathew panicking, looking at the door to the apartment again and no longer worried about how much money he could make from English conversations lessons. He wondered whether this might be the end and if he was about to die inside a collapsed building. He realised no one knew where he was and if he was injured nobody would find him or recognise him for days.

'This is a new building,' said Rika in a comforting voice. 'It's very strong and well-supported. Please stay here Matthew-san. I promise this is the safest place.'

Rika turned her back on Matthew and he watched her open a cupboard beside the table and pull out a medium sized cardboard box. As she opened it he was relieved to see it was an emergency survival kit for earthquakes and he was comforted by the fact he was with a Japanese woman who knew what she was doing.

As the room started to jostle up and down for the next thirty seconds, Rika began holding up items from the box one by one, smiling as calmly as she could as she did so, trying to reassure Matthew. First she showed him a first aid kit, and he nodded and smiled a very crooked smile as she showed him how well prepared she was. Rika also pulled out candles, matches, cotton gloves and a battery-operated flashlight but just as she pulled out some bottled water all the rattling and swaying stopped.

'Everything should be okay now,' said Rika as if she'd been confident all along that nothing really bad would happen, but Matthew felt like his bones were rattling inside him and he continued to hold onto the leg of the table, thinking that if he let go there would be another earthquake.

'Shall we sit up at the table again?' suggested Rika.

'I think I'd like to stay here for a few minutes,' replied Matthew.

'Is this the first time you've ever experienced an earthquake?' Rika asked him.

'Yes,' replied Matthew. 'I didn't realise an earthquake could be this bad.'

'It's going to be okay,' said Rika. Her face showed Matthew she was genuinely concerned about him.

Matthew could see Rika felt awkward staying stooped under the table but he couldn't help thinking to himself that if he left this shelter somehow the slightest movement might trigger another earthquake.

Rika understood and not knowing what else to do, she stayed kneeling beside Matthew and began showing him what else she had in her emergency box. She held up a notepad and pen, some headache tablets, as well as some cash in an envelope. She even held out a miniature bottle of Suntory Scotch Whisky and offered it to Matthew but he declined, trying his best to smile at her as he shook his head.

'I also have emergency food . . . do you call these rations?' she asked him with a smile.

'Yes,' said Matthew, his professional tone of voice returning slowly now.

Rika also pulled out wasabi peas, some chocolate Pocky sticks and a packet of Hi-chew melon-flavoured candy but when she showed Matthew a can of Kikkoman curry sauce with chicken and vegetables his body stopped trembling and he was more interested in looking at this meal in a can. Slowly most of Matthew's fear melted away and he too wanted to get out from under the table and back onto the chair.

Rika went to the refrigerator, took out two cans of Boss iced-coffee and brought them over to where Matthew was sitting. They pulled open the drinks and they started to resume their lesson at the table. Matthew was still a bit shaken but thoughts of his need for extra money quickly returned and it was not long before they were laughing and talking in a much more relaxed manner.

At five p.m. Rika handed Matthew an envelope. When he looked inside he saw that it contained ¥20,000.

'I've only taught you for two hours. You've paid me too much,' he said to Rika.

'But you'll return on Sunday, won't you?' asked Rika, afraid Matthew had been too frightened by the earthquake and he had no plans to return to her apartment on the fourteenth floor.

'I'll definitely return on Sunday,' replied Matthew in the most confident voice he could muster, hoping he sounded nonchalant even though he knew his hands were still quite shaky and his stomach still felt like jelly. He was ashamed Rika had seen him so frightened earlier on. He vowed to himself as he prepared to leave Rika's home that he would never behave like that again but deep down he knew the fear of impending earthquakes would always be at the back of his mind while he was living in Japan.

Matthew returned to Hiroo Station by himself. Rika had offered to walk with him but he knew he'd easily find his way back and he was worried she'd feel that it was necessary to escort him back to the station every week if she accompanied him to the train station that afternoon.

Matthew's stomach was still churning from the earthquake earlier that day as he returned to his home in Roppongi but he didn't find this entirely disagreeable. The strong tremors, the bond he shared with Rika under the table in her apartment and the relief when it was all over, made Matthew feel really excited about Tokyo and he was full of adrenalin. Instead of leaving Matthew frightened and wanting to return to England, he realised that he appreciated Japan even more. No other country had ever made him feel so alive and it was from that day onwards that Matthew knew he'd completely regained his passion for life.

Time has Wings

It was just before four thirty p.m. on a Thursday afternoon in March. The Earl Grey tea was brewing in my finest Wedgwood Wild Strawberry teapot, the matching Wedgwood sugar bowl and two sets of cups and saucers were set out on the dining table and I was busy placing a selection of pastries and cream tarts on a two tier cake stand as I waited for Mrs Nicholls, my next door neighbour, to arrive. She was the only neighbour to come over and introduce herself when we first moved in four years ago. We always met at my house because she lived with five cats and they gave me an allergic reaction. I'd just received a telephone call from my husband and he'd told me some life changing news that I wanted to share with Mrs Nicholls but I was afraid my poor English wouldn't allow me to explain the situation properly.

My children, Daisuke aged twelve and Asuka aged nine, were upstairs in their bedrooms completing their homework and I was fretting downstairs. I was always worrying about whether my English was grammatically incorrect, if my words sounded strange or if a literal translation which was perfectly appropriate in Japanese was conveyed awkwardly and in turn completely misunderstood when I spoke English. I didn't want Mrs Nicholls to feel offended by my wrong choice of words. I'd be mortified if a series of misplaced sentences made me look insincere and incapable of understanding and adapting to the Australian culture, or if my poor English jeopardised my cherished friendship with Mrs Nicholls. From the very first day my family and I had moved into this large and comfortable house in Brighton, Mrs Nicholls had welcomed me into her world with a warmth and kindness that I would never forget and if she misinterpreted me today as I told her my news, I would inevitably feel terrible.

Although I was wearing a pink cashmere turtleneck sweater over my camel jeans, there was a chill in the room so after I'd finished laying the table, I turned the heater on to a low setting. I looked at my watch and I decided I had time to flick through *The Age* newspaper. I understood most of the headlines but even after four years in Australia, I still had trouble understanding all the articles and stories. Now and again, I'd ask my children to translate an article for me, as their English skills were so much better than mine. I did have a tutor who visited me once a week to practise English conversation, but for me this was more of an interest to fill up my free time rather than a serious lesson. I regretted the fact I had not been more diligent in my English studies. So many of the other Japanese wives who lived in Australia had an impressive command of the English language and I was filled with envy when I watched them casually chatting away with Australians while I would always stand in the background, too afraid to dive into the conversations. I'd accepted long ago I was never going to have the right skills to pick up the English language. The task just seemed so incredibly daunting.

I gave up trying to read the front page, placed the newspaper to one side and looked around my well organised, comfortable and spacious living room and smiled as the autumn sun outside shone onto the right side of my face. I thought that despite the fact I'd never been a great English speaker, my family and I had enjoyed some wonderful times in Australia. We lived close to the sea in Brighton, so nearly every weekend in the summer, the children and I, sometimes accompanied by my husband, would go for long walks on the beach. We'd also become involved in lots of sports in Australia. I played tennis once a week with a few of the other Japanese ladies. The children had taken swimming lessons for a year and they loved spending time in the swimming pool in the back garden. My husband's golf had also considerably improved and even I could swing a golf club without embarrassment.

We'd spent a lot more time together as a family since arriving in Australia. My husband had always returned home after eleven p.m. in Japan but in Australia he was often home early. This meant we could always eat dinner together at about seven thirty p.m. Once a month on a Sunday, we'd all go out for a nice, reasonably priced dinner at a restaurant in the city and in January my husband took us all out to a very posh French restaurant for my birthday.

All of these experiences and more would soon come to an end. My husband had called to tell me his manager had announced earlier that day that we'd be returning permanently to Japan in just six weeks. For years, I'd been saying how much I missed my family in Tokyo and all the little things in Japan that I could not get or experience in Australia. Now we were leaving our adopted country, not knowing whether we'd ever return to Australia again, I felt sad and I didn't really want to leave.

The doorbell rang and broke my thoughts. I stood up and walked to the front door. It was lovely to see Mrs Nicholls' smiling face as I welcomed her in.

'Hello Checko, how are you?' Mrs Nicholls asked me as she removed her cream two-inch heels and slipped on a pair of our house slippers. I smiled hearing her mispronounce my name for the hundredth time. She'd never been able to pronounce my name, Chieko, properly.

'I'm fine thank you. How are you?' I asked her, waiting for her usual lengthy and amusing response.

'I'm good Checko...you're not going to believe the news I have to share with you,' said Mrs Nicholls as she followed me in to the dining room table and sat down in front of the cake selection. 'I was at the dry cleaners yesterday and I ran into Jenny Matthews who lives at number thirty-nine.'

I smiled at Mrs Nicholls, lifted the teapot and poured her a cup of tea. I knew she didn't take milk but she always added a couple of sugars. I watched her take two sugar cubes and stir them into her tea as I poured myself a cup. Mrs Nicholls was a slim woman in her early forties and she always looked glamorous. Today was no exception. I admired her beautiful pearl earrings and her silk blouse. She had a bright complexion and laugh lines around her eyes. I could tell she had some exciting news to share about Jenny Matthews and although I'd never met the woman I'd seen her in her front garden and I was keen to hear what Mrs Nicholls had to say. She had a mischievous glint in her eye that told me it was gossip worth hearing.

'Jenny was picking up her dry cleaning and I was dropping mine off,' Mrs Nicholls continued before stopping again for a second to catch her breath and take a sip of tea. 'I asked her how she was and whether her son was doing well. You've seen Jenny and the young man, who lives with her at number thirty-nine, haven't you?'

'Yes, I've seen them both,' I replied. I was keen to hear Mrs Nicholls' news but I was still nervous about how I was going to break the news of our departure to her.

'I'd say Jenny would be about forty-five years old and the boy looks like he's not a day older than twenty-five. Don't you agree?'

'Yes, I think you're right,' I said as I contemplated whether I should just blurt out we would be returning to Japan in six weeks or start talking about how much I enjoyed our friendship and slowly break the news to Mrs Nicholls.

'So Jenny told me that he's not her son,' said Mrs Nicholls, pausing for dramatic effect.

'Who is he?' I asked.

'It's her boyfriend!' she replied.

We both broke into a fit of giggles. This was the basis of our friendship. I understood Mrs Nicholls and she understood me. Mrs Nicholls would share her gossip, always in good humour and without a hint of malice, and I would chuckle and nod along, relishing each moment and later missing Mrs Nicholls and her big personality every time she left the house. Her booming laughter filled every crevice of my living room when she was sitting in it and I was always amused by the way she would heartily throw her arms about as she told each story. It was as if she was bringing the living room to life with her enthusiasm. We both shared an understanding that the world was a funny place and all the little things that worried most people were never to be taken too seriously. I was certainly going to miss my weekly conversations with Mrs Nicholls and listening to her amusing anecdotes.

My son Daisuke appeared at the bottom of the stairs to our right. 'Okaasama, I've finished my homework so can I watch television now?' he asked me, speaking in English for the sake of Mrs Nicholls.

'Have you studied your Japanese kanji characters today?' I asked.

'No,' he replied. He turned and headed back upstairs dragging his feet with each step, complaining under his breath.

'Your children speak English very well,' commented Mrs Nicholls. 'They even have an Australian accent.'

'Yes, you're right' I replied. Daisuke and Asuka had both picked up the language very quickly and their English was much better than mine. They'd both taken after their father, in that they'd had no trouble learning the English language and they had been quick to embrace the Australian culture, but I couldn't tell Mrs Nicholls how worried I was about their Japanese language skills. Daisuke and Asuka would probably struggle when they returned to Japan. Even though they'd attended the Japanese school in Melbourne every Saturday without fail, it would not be enough for them to fit in easily into the Japanese school system when they returned to Tokyo. I was afraid their understanding of Japanese grammar and their limited knowledge of Japanese kanji characters would mean they'd have a difficult time at their new schools in Japan.

'I have something to tell you,' I blurted out without thinking, to my good friend Mrs Nicholls. 'We're returning to Japan in May.' The words had escaped from my mouth without me realising it. Usually I would sit and torment myself over and over, trying to think of a way to say each English sentence in the best way possible, but for some reason today the words came spilling out of me.

'For another holiday?' Mrs Nicholls asked.

'No,' I replied. 'It's a permanent move.'

'I'm going to miss you,' Mrs Nicholls said kindly.

I was sure I could see tears welling up in the corner of her eyes. It was nice to see she was physically affected by my news and I could sense that she would miss me as much as I'd miss her.

'I always enjoy our chats on Thursday afternoons and no one else serves me tea in such lovely Wedgwood fine bone china,' continued Mrs Nicholls.

'I miss you too,' I said with sincerity.

'You mean – I will miss you too,' she said, gently correcting my English.

'Sorry,' I said laughing at my mistake. 'I will miss you too.'

I poured us a second cup of tea and sat back to listen to Mrs Nicholls as she talked about her daughter's upcoming wedding in September, a new Chinese restaurant that had opened in Brighton and later about her holiday to Queensland that she was planning for December. Neither of us wanted to talk about my family's return to Japan and we avoided the subject to save both of us from becoming too emotional. After about forty-five minutes Mrs Nicholls stopped chatting to finish her tea and I picked up a present from the seat next to me which I'd prepared for her earlier that day.

'Thank you for being such a good friend and neighbour,' I said to her as I passed her the gift. These words I'd prepared in my mind earlier and as I handed her the present I hoped Mrs Nicholls could truly feel my sincerity. I wished at that moment that this was a birthday present and not a going away present. I suddenly realised that soon I would be sitting in my living room in Japan and Mrs Nicholls would be on the other side of the world. Even international telephone calls would not be able to replace the moments we had shared over the last few years, laughing and gossiping as we sat together in my Australian living room. Mrs Nicholls eagerly accepted the present and carefully undid the wrapping. She was very pleased to see I'd given her a set of handkerchiefs embroidered with traditional Japanese patterns.

'They're lovely, thank you Checko,' she said to me.

The next ten minutes of conversation were awkward and stilted in the realisation these shared afternoons would all be over in just a few weeks. Finally, we both stood up and headed for the front door. My husband would be home in a couple of hours and Mrs Nicholls knew I'd have to start preparing dinner.

'I'll see you next week at the same time,' said Mrs Nicholls as she put on her shoes and opened the door.

'Yes, I'll see you next Thursday,' I replied. I waited until she reached the front gate before I closed the door.

I sighed and went back into the living room to clear away the Wedgwood fine china and the cakes. I picked them all up carefully, carried them into the kitchen and set them to one side. I'd decided we'd have a Japanese style Vermont curry for dinner that evening and I began preparing the rice for steaming in the rice cooker. I gently folded the rice in the water, drained it and repeated the process until the water was clear. As I finished cleaning the rice I couldn't help thinking of our imminent return to Japan in May. Time had passed so quickly in this country. Given the opportunity, I'd easily spend another four years in Australia. But that was not to be.

* * *

After our return to Japan, I spent the next twelve months integrating myself and my family back into the Japanese way of life. As I predicted, Daisuke and Asuka had a difficult time keeping up with the other Japanese students at school. My husband was busier than ever at work and he was now arriving home after midnight most evenings. Mrs Nicholls called me twice on the telephone but both times our conversations were awkward and stilted. Now that I was no longer surrounded by everything in English, it was even harder for me to translate and explain our present situation to her in English. I tried to sound bright and upbeat on the phone but it was obvious to both of us that we were now living in completely separate worlds. I really did miss Mrs Nicholls and I would often think back to how much we'd laugh and joke during our weekly gossip sessions as I did the ironing or as I was picking up ingredients for dinner at the local supermarket near our new home in Tokyo. I highly doubted whether we would ever return to Australia and I realised my friendship with Mrs Nicholls would never be properly rekindled. As I organised my family life and we all readjusted back into the Japanese way of living, I vowed to myself that I would never forget my good fortune for being able to experience four years in Australia and I would cherish the memories of the good times our family shared in Victoria which was now on the other side of the world. I knew I'd always be thankful for the opportunity to meet such wonderful people in this land – a country which would from now on and forever more gradually become more and more distant and foreign to me, but a place full of delightful memories.

Ginza Girl

I'd studied English in high school and even though my teachers had all been Japanese, I'd always thought that my English conversation level was quite good until one day in August. I'd been overseas a few times and I'd never had any trouble using English to buy new clothes in department stores like Bergdorf Goodman in New York or Harrods in London and I could always find my way to famous tourist attractions like The Colosseum in Rome or the Eiffel Tower in Paris, when I was travelling through Europe.

It was the second Thursday afternoon in August during a shopping trip in Ginza with my friends from work, Chizuru and Hanako, when I discovered my English proficiency was really not as good as I'd always thought.

Chizuru and Hanako were about the same age as me and we shared a mutual appreciation of fashion. Not the Lolita or Gothic Aristocrat styles from Harajuku, we were much more high-end. We were addicted to top designer labels such as Prada, Cartier, Chloé, Diane von Fürstenberg, Issey Miyake and Yohji Yamamoto. Basically, the three of us adored all the haute-couture designers from the chic and very expensive boutiques in Minami Aoyama and Ginza. We were addicted to labels and proud of our lavish wardrobes and our luxurious and vast shoe collections.

On this second Thursday in August when everyone in Tokyo was out and about enjoying the sunshine, Chizuru, Hanako and I were in Ginza, sifting through the latest summer styles in our favourite boutiques, when we decided to stop and eat lunch at the French café-bakery called Aux Bacchanales. It was three p.m. and the café was crowded and lively. We noticed as soon as we sat down that two very glamorous foreign girls were sitting at the table next to us on our right. They looked like models with their deer-like long limbs, their lustrous thick, blonde hair and their smooth, perfect complexions. They were laughing and giggling as they threw back their glossy golden locks. My friends and I watched them with a mixture of awe and bewilderment as they put on quite a performance, posing and preening as if they were auditioning for a sensational film noir. I noticed that the Japanese men sitting at the adjoining tables were also watching them with mouths wide open. The foreign girls stopped their chatter only to sip from their glasses of Perrier mineral water, to check their iPhones for messages or to take out their lipsticks from their beautiful leather Prada and Michael Kors' handbags and apply the rich colours to their lips. Chizuru, Hanako and I tried to guess which country they were from and I said I thought they were from France but Chizuru and Hanako were sure that they were British. My friends teased me for not being able to tell the difference between the English and French languages. Hanako half-heartedly suggested we should interrupt them and ask them where they were from but we all knew the three of us didn't possess the right kind of confidence to initiate a conversation with such intriguing and slightly intimidating foreigners.

Ironically, when we'd finished eating our lunch and we were preparing to leave the French café, one of the two blonde foreign girls lightly tapped Hanako on the shoulder.

'Excuse me,' said the taller foreign girl in very polished and polite English, 'Do you know where we can find the Printemps Department Store in Ginza?'

I completely went blank and didn't know what to say. Even though I'd understood the question, I couldn't form the appropriate answer in English and I blushed deeply at my own uselessness. Chizuru and Hanako, on the other hand, answered back in crisp and perfect English with a confidence I obviously didn't possess and they gave clear and exact directions to the Printemps Department Store which was not far from the café. Hanako's and Chizuru's English ability was so fluent that after the first couple of sentences, I couldn't understand a word they were saying. It all just sounded like gibberish to me. Towards the end of their conversation, I watched in amazement as Chizuru and Hanako exchanged phone numbers with the foreign girls and they promised to meet up with them. The only part I did understand was that sometime in the future they were all planning to go shopping together in Ginza. To further my embarrassment, I found out later the foreign girls were in fact British.

Fifteen minutes later, I made my excuses to Chizuru and Hanako and headed for home. My head was thumping and I was bursting with humiliation. I'd travelled to London, Paris, Rome, New York and Sydney and I'd managed to find my way around all these cities without any problems at all, but I realised that day that a few simple phrases such as "I'd like to buy this" and

"Could I please have a sandwich?" would not suffice if I wanted to have a real conversation with people from English speaking countries.

As I sat on the train on my way home, reading Mixi messages on my iPhone, I was seriously considering the possibility of applying for a twelve-month working holiday visa in London, when I received a text message from Hanako.

[Hi Sachiko, how would you like to join Chizuru and I for English conversation lessons with April at the Better English Language School in Ginza?]

I suddenly realised why Chizuru and Hanako spoke English so fluently but although I read the message three times I couldn't understand the [with April] part. We were now in August and I wondered whether they wanted me to wait eight months before I joined their class. Despite the misunderstanding, I sent back a text message:

[Thank you, I'd love to join your English conversation classes]

I spent the rest of my train journey content in the fact my English may very soon be just as good as Hanako and Chizuru and it wasn't long before I forgot all about the [with April] part of the text message. I was really pleased to receive an invitation from Hanako and Chizuru and I couldn't wait to join them at the Better English Language School in Ginza for conversation classes. Hanako called me the following Monday to tell me she'd managed to enlist me in the same class as her and Chizuru at an intermediate language level and that they met once a week on a Wednesday evening. Even though I'd protested at first that I wouldn't be able to keep up with them or understand such an advanced class, Hanako reassured me several times that within a couple of months I'd be able to catch up and match their English fluency.

I was told the English conversation class would start at six p.m.

On Wednesday evening, after a thirty-minute meeting from five thirty p.m. with the administration staff who had me fill out a number of forms and pay by credit card for six months of conversation classes at the Ginza branch of the Better English Language School; Chizuru, Hanako and myself joined five other Japanese students outside the cubicle marked 'April' on the third floor. When I saw the sign 'April' I didn't say anything to Hanako or Chizuru because I didn't want to appear ignorant again, though at that time I assumed the classrooms were individually marked with the months of the year in English.

At exactly six p.m., a shrill alarm bell rang to mark the start of all the classes. Suddenly, a very tall and painfully thin girl, with flaming red hair and a face covered in freckles, stepped out of the elevator. Hanako told me she was our teacher. Her polyester black suit, her white linen shirt with its extremely long and pointy collar and her scuffed black platform shoes with pink laces, told me this teacher had no interest in fashion and no idea about style. However, she did have a huge and mischievous smile and a welcoming expression which told me this English conversation class might be a lot of fun.

Inside the cubicle which acted as our classroom, once everyone sat down, the red-headed teacher turned to me and I thought she was trying to tell me her name was April. Despite this introduction, I was so nervous to be in such an advanced English class that I didn't ask the teacher to repeat what she'd just told me and I was left wondering whether this interesting looking teacher had actually told me her name or she'd just explained the classroom was called April and I should know that for future reference. I kept thinking it would be strange to call yourself *Shigatsu*, the Japanese equivalent for April, so I decided to just nod and agree with this teacher throughout the lesson. After this, I was quite pleased with myself for clearly understanding the next fifteen minutes of the English class even though I was too nervous to initiate any conversation. The teacher and a couple of the male students were talking about the different languages spoken in other countries and I was just starting to feel confident about my English when the topic suddenly changed again and I had trouble understanding most of the conversation for the remaining twenty minutes of the class. I just continued to smile and nod in unison with everyone else, hoping no-one would notice I was having so much difficulty understanding what the rest of the class was saying.

After forty-five minutes of intense English conversation, I was relieved the class had finally finished but I'd made a silent promise to myself a few minutes earlier that I'd attend every week until my English had greatly improved. As we headed towards the elevator, Chizuru and Hanako introduced me to three of the Japanese boys who had also been in our class. Their names were Hikaru, Junichi and Minoru. I was relieved everyone had reverted back to speaking Japanese and I was very pleased to meet such good-looking young men. I thought Minoru, in particular, was the most attractive and I liked the warm feeling I felt when he put his hand on my elbow to guide me into the elevator and the way he turned around to smile at me as we descended to the ground floor of the building. I'd think of his smile many times over the next seven days until the next class. I'd never seen anyone smile at me with eyes like that which made me feel like we were the only two people in the elevator, although we were surrounded by our friends. He made me feel so alive and in the moment and it was as if time had slowed down as we descended from one floor to the next. He must have noticed my face flush as I held onto his gaze a little longer than I should have. His eyes had a certain familiarity and tenderness to them I hadn't seen before in any another boy and I instantly knew that Minoru was someone who I wanted to get to know. He was a lot taller than me and I had to look up at him. I realised I was up on my tiptoes – it was as if his eyes were tugging up my whole body towards his kind face. Minoru and I were at the very back of the elevator together. My friends who were standing in front with their backs to us wouldn't have noticed this romantic moment I'd just shared with Minoru. My knees were a bit shaky and I had butterflies in my stomach when the door of the elevator finally opened onto the street and the buzz and charm of the Ginza metropolis stretched out before us.

When it was decided we should all go out for coffee, I was the first to agree and I was really looked forward to the next couple of hours, hoping I'd get the chance to get to know Minoru a little bit better.

I followed the group to a Le Café Doutor coffee shop on the same street as the Better English Language School and it soon became clear to me that the group had already spent many evenings there after their English classes and they were all firm friends. As I was new to the group, I couldn't overcome the usual shyness which I always felt when I met new people. When the coffees arrived, Hanako and Chizuru started to talk with the boys about our teacher and it was then I realised her name was actually April. As I sat sipping my mocha iced coffee, I heard Chizuru ask the boys whether they thought our teacher was attractive. Hikaru replied that he didn't think she was very pretty but she had a good personality and in a hushed tone he revealed that he knew that April had a boyfriend because he'd seen them out together on a date. Obviously, all of us wanted to know more about this boyfriend and we urged Hikaru to go on and explain. He told us he was with Minoru in Ginza earlier in the week on Monday and they'd seen April inside a popular teishoku restaurant at lunchtime, sitting with a Japanese man who looked like he was at least fifty years old. Hikaru went on to say they'd instantly recognised April because of her striking red hair and they'd also seen her face at the end of his meal when they went to pay at the counter. Hikaru must have enjoyed the fact we were all enthralled by this topic and so he continued. He sat back and slowly explained in a low voice that April and her Japanese male friend had been very friendly towards each other. He said they'd both leant across the table several times for a quick kiss on the lips and April had placed her hand on the Japanese man's arm continuously throughout their meal.

We all sat back in silence for a minute or so, all of us completely taken aback by this revelation. Minoru confirmed that without a doubt April and the Japanese man were obviously dating. I'd lost a bit of my shyness by this time and I asked Minoru whether he'd noticed if

April usually wore a wedding band. Minoru smiled warmly back at me and shook his head slowly from side to side for effect, showing us without a word that April wasn't married, but we gasped in disbelief when Minoru went on to explain that the Japanese man had in fact been wearing a wedding ring and he smiled when he saw a look of shock pass over each of our faces when we realised April was dating a married man. This new information left us all absolutely flabbergasted and we were hardly able to contain ourselves as we all fell into a fit of giggles, but a few coughs and stares from the two septuagenarians at the next table brought us back to our senses. Chizuru quickly changed the subject and we spent the rest of the evening much calmer talking about our travels to other countries and a popular drama on television which we all liked to watch.

I continued with the English conversation classes throughout the summer and well into the autumn and winter and slowly my English conversation proficiency improved but my listening skills were still much better than my ability to speak English with any confidence. Every Wednesday, I hoped Minoru would ask me out on a date but he was just as shy as me. Although I wanted to spend some time alone with him, it was nice to get to know him with my friends around and in a way the group situation allowed us to get to know each other a lot better without the awkwardness we may have felt if we were by ourselves.

It was one Wednesday evening in December when it was bitterly cold outside that Chizuru, Hanako and I rushed into the Better English Language School and took the elevator for the third floor, chatting about what we'd bought earlier that day from the Mitsukoshi

Department Store in Ginza. We met up with Hikaru, Junichi and Minoru who were standing in front of the elevator on the third floor and we all waited with the other students for April to arrive to open the door to the classroom.

At six p.m. as the siren rang for the start of the class, April stepped out of the elevator and we all turned to welcome her. It was clearly apparent to all of us that April was not her usual self. Her hair was tied back nicely and she was dressed in her familiar unfashionable and cheap looking black polyester suit, but her eyes were bloodshot and her expression was clearly strained. A black cloud seemed to hover above her as April walked towards us without a word and opened up the classroom. We all silently filed in behind her and sat down not knowing what to say. Our teacher told us with a stutter that we were going to talk about relationships in English that evening and how relationships could be very good but they could also be very bad. A tear slid down her cheek as she said the word "relationships". None of us knew what to do and we all just stared at April with expressions of concern. Our teacher, who usually stood so tall and confident, fell into her chair and covered her face as she began to sob and apologise for her behaviour at the same time. Hanako stood up and approached her cautiously. We all knew Hanako had a maternal side to her and she would not make matters worse and she clearly just wanted to offer some form of consolation as she placed a gentle hand on April's shoulder and squatted beside her chair and handed her a tissue. April accepted it with gratitude as she explained to us all that her "much older and unappreciative boyfriend" had broken up with her and he'd also told her he never wanted to see her again. We all sat staring at each other for a few minutes before Junichi decided he was going to help to defuse the situation. He stood up and almost took over the class with his authoritarian manner. He started to talk about his sister's ex-boyfriend. He told us how this man had been so nasty and cruel to his sister and he'd completely humiliated her on several occasions. April looked up from her chair at Junichi and as she listened to him her sobs turned into empathy and later into encouragement. By the end of the class, April's normally bright and friendly personality had returned. After the lesson, it was Chizuru who invited April to join us at the Le Café Doutor for coffee that evening and some friendly companionship. There were seven of us who left the Better English Language School that evening and the staff who worked in administration on the first floor were happy to see us all leave so animated and chirpy.

As we were walking from the language school to the coffee shop, Minoru pulled me to one side and asked if I'd like to have dinner with him on the following Friday. I accepted straight away, trying not to look too enthusiastic even though I felt like fireworks were going off inside me. We were now good friends and I knew there would be no awkwardness or uneasiness on our first date. As the evening progressed, Minoru and I shared many smiles with each other and I was so happy I'd decided to learn English and I'd met such a wonderful young man. When I told Hanako and Chizuru that Minoru and I were going out together on Friday, they were really pleased for me. Hanako told me she'd actually encouraged Minoru to ask me out. Both of my friends had known that Minoru and I would be a perfect match but we were both too shy to move the relationship forward so Hanako had taken it upon herself to offer Minoru a few words of encouragement. I gave Hanako an appreciative hug before we parted that evening and she promised to help me pick out an outfit for my date with Minoru on Friday.

While I was returning home on the train thinking about everything that had happened to me that day, I thought to myself that I was the luckiest girl in the world for having such wonderful friends and I knew that without a doubt Minoru would be the perfect boyfriend. My life was getting better and better and I couldn't have been happier.

A Wife for Kurou

My auntie brought up the idea of an arranged marriage. She talked about this in detail with my parents for about six months until they'd all finally agreed this would be the best way for me to find the ideal wife. I didn't really have much to say in the matter but this didn't bother me at all. My life had been planned out for me by my parents since I was a small child and the idea of an arranged marriage seemed like a very natural and normal progression for me.

I'd just turned thirty and although my family would often reassure me I was a very good-looking, young man and highly intelligent, I'd never met a girl who I'd even begin to consider suitable enough to call my wife.

My father held the highly esteemed position of deputy general manager at the Nippon Steel & Sumitomo Metal Corporation and he'd always had high hopes that I being his only child would continue in his footsteps and become an important part of this well-respected company. From the day I was born, I'd been raised to be just like my father and to fulfil all his wishes for me to become an integral part of the management structure at the company for whom he worked and naturally I was a willing participant in my parents' decisions. I grew up shadowing my father, desperate to emulate him and become just as successful.

Up until the time when my family began discussing the possibility of an arranged marriage, I'd been so totally absorbed in climbing the corporate ladder with the help and encouragement of my father that I'd never really thought about when I was going to find a wife or raise a family. I'd attended cram schools from the age of eight and I'd studied over ten hours a day for years on end in order to be accepted at Keio University. After graduating with a Master's Degree, I'd very proudly accepted an offer from the Nippon Steel & Sumitomo Metal Corporation to work at their Marunouchi branch with my father. I'd thrown myself into my job with on-going encouragement and guidance from my father and I'd done remarkably well at work over the past six years, rising quickly from a junior position and for a long time working successfully in various departments. I'd simultaneously built strong alliances within my own company and close ties with executives from other companies. My father was extremely proud of me and he would often tell me so. He loved to hear from his colleagues how his son was exemplary in the way he'd always follow procedures, how much they admired the fact that I'd often work later than any other person in the office, how I'd never take unnecessary risks, and how I was always cautious when it came to decision making. It pleased me to see my father brimming with pride as he spoke to the other managers about my loyalty to the company and being aware of this, I was happy to please my father who'd always been someone who I'd highly admired.

Although I was a diligent worker, there were moments when I thought about rebelling against the other managers and I didn't always agree with some of the decisions they made, but I knew I'd have to wait until I held a much more senior position when I was about forty-five or fifty years old before I could start to suggest some of the more modern and innovative ideas that I had for the future of the company. Until that time I'd decided I would completely dedicate myself to the status quo and conform every day to the wishes of my senior managers.

Many of my colleagues had girlfriends or wives and it was not the case that I'd never thought about women or dating. I could envisage myself being matched to a sensible but caring girl in the future but she would have to be intelligent, beautiful, and supportive and from an excellent family who had the right social status. I'd sometimes think about asking out some of the girls who worked in the office but after observing each of them for a period of time, I'd always came to the same conclusion – they were not well-educated or attractive enough for my liking.

In January, my auntie presented me with a small photo of a very beautiful girl called Tomiko Yukimoto. In the picture she was dressed in an elaborate kimono. I was told she'd been chosen from a number of girls because of her family's good reputation, the fact she also spoke Chinese as well as English and because she'd attended Keio University just like me, although she'd graduated three years later. I was pleased to find out she'd also seen my photo and she was looking forward to meeting me.

I'd admired the photo at length for at least thirty minutes before agreeing with my auntie to meet Tomiko and her parents for a preliminary meeting, which was hastily arranged.

During the first very formal introduction, I only had the chance to talk to Tomiko for a couple of minutes but after this first meeting my parents and I were excited to meet with Tomiko and her family again and to see whether we were well suited and if she'd make a fine wife for me. Tomiko and I only shared a couple of words but I was pleased to observe that she and her family were very polite. Tomiko was certainly very beautiful and I liked her style of dressing. Her clothes were very stylish and well-made. She'd worn a beige silk dress for our first introduction with a string of pearls around her long and swan-like neck. Tomiko also had thick, jet-black hair that curled nicely around her shoulders and I'd noticed her feet were very small. I'd always liked girls with very small feet. I'd seen girls with feet a lot bigger than Tomiko and for some reason which I could not explain I didn't like the idea of marrying a woman with big feet.

During our second meeting, I was able to spend more time with Tomiko but it was during our brief one hour conversation when I started to have second thoughts about whether she would be the perfect wife and the ideal match for me. I'd spent my whole life constantly aiming for perfection. I'd always been at the top of my class, I'd always been bought the best of everything and as an only child I was used to getting whatever I wanted from my parents who did not like to see me ever go without. I considered myself to be a rising star at the Nippon Steel & Sumitomo Metal Corporation and I didn't want my colleagues nor my friends to criticize me and think I'd made the wrong choice in my quest to find a wonderful wife and a decent mother for my future children. I wasn't totally egotistical even though

I believed a man should possess a powerful ego if he was going to succeed in life. One part of my personality, which some people called a gift and others called a curse, was that I could always see the imperfections in others. Although my parents both knew I always expected the highest standards from myself and everyone around me, my mother and my father both looked upon this as if it was a positive and not a negative attribute. However, deep down I knew this may be the very trait in my personality that was keeping me from sustaining a long-term relationship with a woman.

After spending just under sixty minutes with Tomiko, I noticed she had a tendency to speak down to me and it was impossible for me to ignore the fact she seemed to possess a haughty and supercilious manner. I was three years older than her but she spoke to me as if I was a lot younger and as if there was absolutely no chance of me being able to understand her esoteric way of thinking. I understood Tomiko was very well-educated and every time I saw her I couldn't help but admire the fact she was exquisitely good-looking and very refined but I didn't like feeling at all that she somehow felt I was inferior to her.

A third meeting was arranged by my auntie and my parents and this time I wasn't looking forward to seeing Tomiko again. She made my heart palpitate and my palms sweaty and I had a prevailing sense of unease about meeting her and her family for the third time. I started having trouble sleeping through the night and I was a little more distracted than usual at work. I was beginning to wonder if I should postpone the meeting with Tomiko, and I had thoughts of gradually easing her out of my life until the time came when I could find someone who didn't make me wake up in a cold sweat, but simultaneously I was strangely drawn to her.

One day, when I realised I'd been thinking about Tomiko for a full fifteen minutes instead of working on an important project at work, I began to wonder if I had the symptoms typical of a man who was starting to fall in love but I immediately rejected this idea as being preposterous and forced myself to concentrate on the job at hand. Over the next few days, I found myself again and again staring into space at my desk during the day, thinking about the way Tomiko pursed her lips just before she spoke or the way she raised one eyebrow when she was thinking about answering a question. I was wondering whether she might be the perfect match if I just gave her another chance, but I still had a nagging feeling I was just wasting my time meeting with Tomiko and her family and I was also worried about Tomiko's supercilious manner. I couldn't talk to my parents about the reservations I was having because my mother and father were both excited about the close friendship they were forming with Tomiko's parents and they were delighted with the developing arrangement. It was all they ever talked about with my auntie. I decided to keep my worries to myself and give the relationship a little more time before I opened up to my mother and father.

It was a very muggy day in the last week in May when both of our families were preparing to meet again. I'd never liked the weather at this time of the year. The tsuyu rainy season would begin soon and I was a person who didn't like the high humidity. I was grumpy on the morning that Tomiko and her family were visiting for lunch at our home and I was particularly bad company at breakfast. My father scolded me for being rude to my mother and I apologized before I excused myself from the table, thinking I would surely be in a much better mood if I didn't have to tolerate Tomiko's arrogant nature later that day. My auntie and my parents, in contrast, were in high spirits as they tidied the house and prepared for the Yukimoto family's arrival. I escaped to my bedroom wishing I could read a book all afternoon instead of meeting with Tomiko.

At exactly one p.m., Tomiko and her parents stepped out of their white luxury sedan. My father and my auntie and I waited silently in the tatami room until we heard the doorbell ring. Just as we heard the front door open, my auntie leaned over to adjust my tie, warning me to be as nice as possible. I had the feeling my auntie suspected I was not entirely thrilled about this situation.

I could hear my mother greeting the Yukimotos at the entrance to our home with a lot of pomp and flourish. My father, my auntie and I all looked up with set smiles across our faces as the partition between the tatami room and the entrance hall slid open and Mr and Mrs Yukimoto entered, followed closely behind by Tomiko and my mother. I couldn't help but notice how radiant Tomiko was looking in a peacock blue coloured silk dress with a pretty floral design embroidered across the front and I liked the way her hair was pulled up in a casual chignon to accentuate the curve of her long neck. Tomiko smiled at my father and my auntie but she completely ignored my gaze as she knelt down between her mother and father in the seiza position with her legs tucked underneath her knees.

My dear mother had prepared chirashizushi with rice, tuna, shiitake mushrooms, prawns and cucumber for lunch. As Tomiko and I ate this delicious meal we didn't speak one word to each other. I couldn't help but think as I slowly and nervously ate each mouthful that I could never truly see myself falling in love with Tomiko. I watched my parents chatter and laugh with Mr and Mrs Yukimoto and for the first time in my life I wished I could defy my mother and father and speak my mind. I wanted to speak from the heart and tell them I thought Tomiko was a bad choice but I didn't have the courage. Instead, I graciously listened to their conversations and nodded along at their remarks but at the same time I wanted to disagree, walk out and escape the situation in which I felt I'd lost complete control.

At the end of the meal, the dishes were taken away and my mother brought in an ashtray for my father and Mr Yukimoto to smoke cigarettes. I didn't smoke but I couldn't help thinking how pleasant it would be if the men retired to one room and the ladies to another. My father offered Mr Yukimoto a cigarette from his packet of Mevius Super Lights without budging or asking the ladies to leave, but Tomiko's father declined, telling everyone at the table that he only ever smoked the Seven Stars brand. We watched Mr Yukimoto reach into his shirt pocket, take out a packet of Seven Stars and turn it upside down but after a few shakes not one cigarette fell out and we realised he'd brought along an empty packet. I suddenly had a brilliant idea which would allow me to disappear for at least thirty minutes to collect my thoughts. I watched my mother with a smug smile as she started to get flustered at the thought that Mr Yukimoto had nothing to smoke when she'd planned such a perfect lunch and I decided that it was my responsibility to rectify the situation. It hadn't escaped my attention during my first and second meeting with Tomiko and her parents that Mr Yukimoto was a heavy smoker and I knew he'd feel very uncomfortable without his cigarettes.

'There's a vending machine that sells cigarettes not far from the house,' I said to my mother as I smiled reassuringly at Mr Yukimoto. 'I'm happy to go and buy Tomiko's father a packet.'

Mr Yukimoto smiled up at me and gave me a nod showing me how much he appreciated my kind gesture. He reached into his trouser pocket to get me some change but I jumped up quickly, refusing repeatedly to take his money, insisting I'd pay for the cigarettes as I shuffled across the tatami mats and opened the sliding partition that separated the tatami room from the hall which led to the entrance of our home. All I could think about was how nice it would be for me to get away from the room and the Yukimotos for half-an-hour. I was thinking about how clever I was when my auntie suddenly interjected and made a suggestion that would dash my hopes of a possible escape.

'I think it would be nice for Tomiko-chan to accompany Kurou-kun,' said my auntie, looking directly up at me and beckoning for me to wait. 'It will give them a chance to spend some time together by themselves.'

Both parents at the table nodded and exchanged knowing smiles as Tomiko slowly rose to her feet. She was blushing deeply and frowning as she approached me. Tomiko gently closed the sliding partition and walked past me as if I wasn't even there before making a beeline for the entrance to put on her shoes. I hesitantly followed her, wishing I'd begged her to rest after such a large meal. I watched her straighten her back and hold her head up high as she slipped into her heels and

I wanted to turn back and let her go by herself but I knew this would be impossible for me to do and it would also be extremely rude.

As Tomiko adjusted her elegant but precariously high pair of four inch heels, it was difficult for me not to admire her small feet again as I stepped into my loafers but as I turned my attention away from her feet I suddenly thought of a cruel way to make her suffer for being so condescending. I knew that if we turned left at the end of the driveway, there was a vending machine that sold cigarettes only five minutes away, however if we turned right it would take about forty minutes to get to another vending machine and back to the house again. I was well and truly aware of the fact the shorter route would mean I wouldn't have to spend too much time in her company but as I watched her wobble towards the end of the drive in her extremely high heels, I couldn't resist the urge to test her patience and tolerance, knowing she would have a difficult time walking in such high heels for longer than a few minutes.

When Tomiko turned around, not knowing which way to turn, I nodded towards the right and began following her at a distance, very much enjoying the maliciously sweet taste of my impending revenge. I knew she would soon start to struggle in those fancy heels.

I kept a distance of about two metres behind Tomiko as we made our way down the rather steep avenue and I watched Tomiko with a satisfied smirk as she tottered carefully along. I couldn't take my eyes off the back of her thighs which constricted tightly as she concentrated on maintaining her balance and I watched with pleasure the way her calf muscles tightened with every step, in her effort to walk naturally. Although I felt a sense of self-satisfaction, for a few seconds I couldn't help but admire her agility and competence walking in heels so high as well as her level of endurance. Tomiko kept her head up, looking from left to right along the avenue for a vending machine. She didn't turn around once to ask me how far we had to walk although she was obviously starting to struggle to maintain her composure in the tiring humidity and under the glare of the oppressive late afternoon sun.

Just before we'd finally reached the vending machine, I watched with delight as Tomiko tripped on a crack in the pavement. It was then I knew I'd exacted my revenge. I thought of all the times she's looked down at me and as she fell over I stopped and stood back to watch her with glee, not wanting to rush up and rescue her at all. I licked my lips, sucked in my breath and crossed my arms with a sense of deep satisfaction as I heard Tomiko emit a short shrill scream as she swayed before crumbling to the ground. Tomiko quickly raised herself back up to a crouching position and began rubbing her left ankle. I was so pleased I'd finally conquered this patronising woman.

I nonchalantly asked Tomiko if she was okay as I quickly passed by her and continued walking towards the vending machine. She stood up straight again with her hands on her hips and angrily pursed her lips together as she watched me casually tip several coins into the vending machine and pull out a packet of Seven Star Charcoal Filter cigarettes for her father. As I came back towards Tomiko and handed her the cigarettes, I deliberately avoided her gaze before brushing past her and heading back towards the house.

About five minutes later, I turned around to check and see if Tomiko was following me but when I did

I saw she was further back than I'd thought. She was covering her eyes and I could see that her shoulders were trembling and tears were running down her face. A wave of pity completely engulfed me and before I had time to think, I hurried back to her, totally forgetting my intention to be as rude as possible. Tomiko looked almost child-like as she sobbed into her palms and for the first time I saw her as a completely different person – a proud girl who was careful not to let strangers into her life too easily and a person who had emotions just like me. When I reached her side, I suddenly felt overwhelmed with guilt and compassion. I could hear Tomiko gasping as she tried to fight back tears and it hit me unexpectedly that I'd been terribly cruel and unkind to a woman who I hardly knew. I crouched down to Tomiko's level and cupped her right hand. As I gently lifted her chin with my index finger and looked into her eyes I caught a vulnerability that I'd never seen before. I suddenly felt an urge to protect and look after Tomiko.

'I'm so sorry,' I said to her gently. 'Are you all right?'

'No,' whispered Tomiko in a soft voice, 'I'm afraid you don't like me at all. You never look at me and smile. Do you think I'm an ugly and horrible person?'

I was shocked. I'd never thought until now about Tomiko's feelings or whether she liked me or if she might be afraid that I didn't like her. I'd only thought about my own future and how I felt about the arranged marriage. I suddenly wanted Tomiko to respect me and like me and as I held her perfectly manicured tiny hand, for the first time I wanted so much for her to think that I might be a suitable husband and not a rude man who was completely unaware of anyone else's feelings.

'I'm really very sorry. I don't think you're ugly at all. In fact, I think you're very beautiful,' I said to Tomiko as I helped her up.

I noticed a taxi driving slowly down the avenue and I waved to the driver, beckoning him to stop. When the driver pulled up and the door of the taxi opened, I guided Tomiko into the back seat and as I sat next to her I held her hand for the duration of the short ride back to my home. When we reached the end of my driveway, I asked the driver to take us up to the door and after the driver had parked directly in front of the entrance I walked around to the other side of the car to help Tomiko onto the pavement adjacent to the door of my home.

'We have a lovely garden with a seat overlooking a pond at the back of the house,' I suggested to Tomiko with the kindest smile I could manage. 'Would you like to sit there with me and watch the carp swimming about for a while before we go back inside?'

'I have to give my father his cigarettes,' Tomiko replied.

'Don't worry; I'll give them to him. I'll meet you in the back garden in a couple of minutes,' I said to Tomiko. 'It's a bit cooler now so I'm going to put on my jacket. Are you cold?'

'No, I'm fine thank you,' said Tomiko. 'I'll wait for you next to the pond.'

She passed me the cigarettes and I watched her walk towards the side of the house, on her way to the back garden, before I opened the front door.

* * *

Thirty minutes later, I noticed my auntie stealthily watching us from behind the kitchen window where she

was washing up the dishes. She quickly glanced at us several times with a knowing smile and I knew she'd be so happy to see the two of us getting along so well. I was sure she'd be delighted to see us chatting and laughing together as we sat side by side on the seat in the garden enjoying each other's company.

I finally felt comfortable next to Tomiko. We were having a lovely time as we watched the carp swimming in the pond in front of us. Without the unspoken barriers that had kept us from getting to know each other properly before, we soon discovered we had a lot in common. I would never again doubt my auntie's matchmaking skills – Tomiko was a terrific girl and she was also very beautiful. I was really looking forward to spending a lot more time with her. Now we were both more relaxed in each other's company, we were able to talk about our dreams and aspirations in a way that suggested we were both thinking about sharing our future together and it all made perfect sense to me.

Valentine's Day Humiliation

'Would you like these chocolates I received for Valentine's Day? I don't want them,' Shin said as he handed a lavish and delicious looking box of individually wrapped chocolates over to his friend Kenta. 'These were on my desk this morning when I arrived at the office.'

'Are the chocolates from that girl called Ami-san who says hello to you every morning and who you do your best to avoid? The ugly girl you told me about a few weeks ago with the thick black glasses who twitches her nose every time she looks up at you?' asked Kenta, as he accepted the box of chocolates with both hands.

Shin was about to reply but he could see Kenta was very pleased to receive the chocolates and he was completely absorbed in reading the small print on the box. He knew Kenta was thinking about opening the box even though he was about to enjoy a large bowl of ramen. When Kenta began to carefully peel the clear plastic wrapping off the box of chocolates, Shin stopped him with a swift slap on his fingertips.

It was a very cold night in mid-February and both men were wrapped up tightly in warm goose down jackets. Although they were both hungry and tired, they were very pleased to see each other. Kenta and Shin were in their twenties and lived in Sakura-Shinmachi. Once a month on a Friday, they'd always meet up at this ramen yatai mobile food station near their apartments at eight o'clock in the evening. Shin and Kenta had grown up together in Nagasaki but they'd both moved to Tokyo for work purposes. Both of them had spent their teens in Kyushu, enjoying late nights drinking beer and eating ramen, yakitori and oden at the yatai food stations in their hometown. Shin always liked to eat miso-based ramen and Kenta preferred the more salty shio-based versions.

The owner of the yatai in Sakura-Shinmachi had been serving Shin and Kenta on a regular basis for just over ten months and the two friends no longer had to place their orders. The owner knew exactly what they liked to eat and in what order he should serve it – drinks first followed quickly by large bowls of their favourite steaming ramen. As soon as Shin and Kenta arrived in the early evening and sat down on one of eight rickety stools in front of the mobile kitchen, the yatai owner would welcome them with the warm and friendly word "*irasshai*" in a booming voice before handing each of them a glass of shōchū served neat. Shin and Kenta enjoyed watching him as he swiftly and expertly prepared large bowls full of delicious ramen noodles that cradled slices of pork belly, poached egg, mushrooms, bamboo shoots and spring onions, all served up in the owner's very special and unique broth.

Kenta was a young man who liked to eat. His whole day revolved around what he planned to have for breakfast, lunch and dinner. He preferred a Western-style breakfast consisting of sugary cereals, French pastries often filled with custard and at least two cups of hot chocolate. At lunchtime, he'd leave his workplace to visit one of the many quick and cheap restaurants he'd been thinking about all morning. Sometimes he'd eat a couple of bowls of noodles, at other times he'd take on the challenge of at least ten plates of conveyor belt sushi and when he was really hungry he could devour three whole hamburgers at the fast-food restaurant Lotteria in one sitting. In the evening, he'd order in large pizzas or tuck into a multitude of ready-meal delights which he'd lug home in large carrier bags from the local convenience store.

In contrast, Kenta's friend Shin was a good-looking, young man who watched his diet carefully, only because he had a lingering fear of getting fat and he relished the attention he received from women wherever he went.

'I'm happy you like the box of chocolates but I think you should wait until after the meal before you open them,' said Shin as he took the box of chocolates from Kenta and placed them on the bench in front of him. 'You know you won't be able to eat just one and yes the chocolates are from Ami-san. I've been working at that office for months now and she still goes out of her way to try to strike up a conversation with me even though I do my best to avoid her,' said Shin. 'I was afraid she might give me something for Valentine's Day and I deliberately arrived at work early this morning so I could hide the gift before the other guys at work turned up and laughed at me. They've been teasing me about Ami-san for weeks. They keep telling me I'm a fool for not asking her out on a date but I'm sure they're just mocking me.' Shin stopped talking but only for a moment so he could take a large slurp of the ramen noodles which had just been placed in front of him. 'You should see her Kenta-kun,' Shin continued.

'She wears the biggest and ugliest pair of thick glasses which completely take over her face and it's difficult to tell whether she's smiling or unhappy because you can't see around the frames. As I've told you before, the glasses slip down her nose all the time and it makes her face twitch constantly. As well as this, her uniform is too big and she always wears a heavily starched white shirt underneath it with the longest and pointiest collar I've ever seen. Her shoes are also too big and the heels are too high so I hear her shuffling around the office. I dare not watch her because I'm afraid she's going to fall over or twist her ankle near my desk and I'll be expected to help her and come to her rescue. If the other guys in the office saw that happen they'd think it was a sign that I'm interested in her.'

Shin stopped talking to eat another mouthful of ramen. It had been a long day at the office, he'd skipped lunch and he'd been looking forward to meeting up with his friend Kenta all day.

After three mouthfuls of ramen noodles, Kenta couldn't help returning his attention to the box of chocolates. 'These chocolates look expensive so I'm sure Ami-san didn't give a box to every man in your office. She has good taste and it seems to me that she thinks you're really special,' said Kenta to his friend Shin, wishing a girl had taken as much trouble to please him on Valentine's Day. All he'd received was a few obligatory chocolates from the older ladies in the office who had handed them out to everyone as a token to mark that special day on February the fourteenth.

Shin had known his friend Kenta would love these chocolates and he wondered whether there would be any left when Kenta finally reached the entrance to his home later that night. Shin knew the chocolates would all be eaten during the fifteen solitary minutes it would take Kenta to walk back to his home after they'd finished eating at the ramen mobile food station and he also knew Kenta would enjoy every one of them.

'I know this chocolate shop,' continued Kenta enthusiastically. 'It's called Mont St Clair and it's famous for its chocolates. You can buy them at their patisserie in Jiyugaoka. It's owned by the celebrity chef called Hironobu Tsujiguchi – it's a very famous shop. I'm really going to enjoy eating these. By the way, are you going to buy Ami-san something for White Day in four weeks?' Kenta teased Shin as he picked up the box of chocolates from the bench in front of them and put them away in his briefcase.

'Of course I'm not going to encourage her and buy her something for White Day,' said Shin in good humour. 'I'm glad Valentine's Day is only once a year because I'm sure Ami-san would buy me a present every day if she could! It's so embarrassing the way she tries to talk with me all the time and if it continues I'm going to have to be really rude to her so she realises I'm not interested.'

'You should ask out one of the other girls in the office and she might stop bothering you if she sees you're going out with someone else,' said Kenta, finding it difficult to change the subject when he found the whole situation between his friend Shin and the ugly girl called Ami extremely amusing.

'The other ladies in the office are all about twenty years older than me, married and in their forties,' said Shin before he ate another mouthful of his ramen.

'That's too bad,' replied Kenta.

'The ramen is delicious,' Shin cried out to the owner of the ramen yatai mobile food station.

The owner smiled and nodded but he did not say a word. He just continued preparing bowls of ramen for two middle-aged men in black overcoats who had arrived shortly after Kenta and Shin.

The two friends ate the rest of their meal in silence. Shin kept thinking about the girl who was bothering him at work and Kenta couldn't stop thinking about the chocolates in his briefcase.

Although Shin and Kenta had both been living in Tokyo for ten months, they'd always revert back to the Kyushu dialect when they met up for ramen and anyone sitting beside them would rarely interrupt their friendly chit-chat. Kenta was a robust man who had spent many years working out in the gym in his teens and the brutal exercise routine he'd adhered to on a daily basis when he was younger had transformed him from a scrawny boy into a much more thick-set fellow. When Kenta had started at university and he'd moved away from the family home, he'd begun partying too much and eating a lot of junk food because he didn't know how to cook. Before long, all his muscle building had wasted away from too many drinks and late nights and he was now a chunky man with a blubbery neck and no waistline who had completely lost the will to take care of the way he looked. The definition in his face had disappeared and if he didn't have a thick head of hair he would have looked just like a giant white marshmallow. Shin had once told Kenta that his balloon-like physique made him look like an orb dressed in a suit that you could easily roll down a hill if you pushed him on to his side.

When Kenta walked down a narrow street other people would have to sidle past him sideways and in the ramen yatai where he was now sitting only seven people instead of eight could sit side by side on the stools due to the fact that Kenta would need the room of two men. No-one ever complained but the owner would sometimes have to ask customers to return later when there would be more room for them to sit down.

Shin, on the other hand, had never followed a gruelling exercise regime although he did like to eat well-balanced meals but only because he was such a vain person and his looks meant everything to him. He was lucky to have a naturally toned physique which many Japanese men envied. He was so attractive women would often stop him in the street to ask for directions and female customer service assistants in department stores would go out of their way to provide him with better service and flash him a friendlier smile than when they served other less eye-catching men. These situations rarely led to more meaningful relationships as Shin would often cut short these pretty women's advances with his arrogance and his indifference. Shin was well aware of his fine attributes and most women fell well below his high expectations.

Since Shin and Kenta had moved to Tokyo, they'd relied on each other for company as they both hardly knew anyone else on this side of Japan. Growing up, Shin and Kenta had built a solid friendship in Kyushu and this was strengthened with each month they spent in Tokyo together. They'd helped each other move into their respective one bedroom apartments in Sakura-Shinmachi and they'd spent many a Friday night in their first full summer in Tokyo looking for casual flings with the sassy American and European girls who liked to party in Roppongi.

Kenta liked going out with Shin because his good looks attracted all the girls and Shin enjoyed being with Kenta because he was overweight and the girls would inevitably choose him at the end of the night. When Shin and Kenta did meet a couple of American or European girls in Roppongi in the summer, they would practise their limited English conversation skills on them and they would applaud each other for each full English question they were able to master. Shin and Kenta would enjoy asking the foreign girls questions in English like, "How long have you been in Tokyo? Do you like Japanese food?" and "Do you like Japanese men?" These questions were repeated on a different set of girls every Friday night with mutual encouragement and much enjoyment from the two boys. Both Kenta and Shin liked chasing foreign girls in the hope of a casual affair and as soon as they arrived in a bar they'd survey the room hoping to strike up a conversation with a couple of young and innocent girls from Europe or America, especially those dressed in provocative outfits who were out in Roppongi doing their best to impress the many Japanese businessmen who were looking for a good time. More often than not, Kenta would end up alone at the end of the night catching the last trains from Roppongi to Shibuya and from Shibuya to Sakura-Shinmachi. Shin, on the other hand, would nearly always leave one of the many bars in Roppongi arm-in-arm with a pretty foreign girl who'd he'd escort to one of the many hotels in the local area. There he'd spend the night with her before sneaking out in the morning after paying the bill and leaving a thank you note by the bed with a fake telephone number on it. If Shin and Kenta were out in Roppongi a week or two later and they ran into one of Shin's dates from the past, they'd always pretend that they suddenly couldn't understand the girl's English and they would make a quick exit from the bar, running as fast as they could to the next bar where they'd collapse on bar stools in fits of laughter.

* * *

Four weeks after Valentine's Day, Shin and Kenta met up at the same ramen yatai mobile food station in Sakura-Shinmachi just after eight p.m. on White Day. The weather was still frosty and they both arrived wearing their coats. Although the air outside was very cold for the fourteenth of March they were both in high spirits as they sat down to eat their favourite ramen in the whole of Tokyo.

'I have to ask,' said Kenta as he took off his gloves and rubbed the palms of his hands together to keep them warm. 'Did Ami-san receive anything for White Day?'

Shin looked down into his glass of shōchū which the owner of the yatai had just passed to him and shook his head from side to side. 'You're not going to believe this,' replied Shin. 'Ryota-kun, who is two years older than me and works two desks away from me at the office, gave her a bunch of white roses and I heard from the other guys that he's taking her out on a date tonight. I can't understand this – I've worked with him for months and he's a really nice and decent guy. He's also very intelligent and he'd have no trouble finding a beautiful girlfriend but he's obviously interested in

Ami-san. I was really surprised to find out he's been thinking about asking her out for months. I honestly don't know why he likes her.'

'Well, that's good news. Ami-san won't be pestering you anymore! Take a look at those two girls sitting next to me,' said Kenta in a low voice, flicking his eyes to the left. 'They're pretty don't you think?'

'Not pretty enough for me,' said Shin with a laugh. He watched the disappointment flare up on Kenta's face when he heard his friend's reaction. 'They're wearing too much make-up and their clothes look cheap,' said Shin.

'You're probably right,' said Kenta in dismay as he glanced over at the two girls one last time, half wishing his friend Shin wasn't there and he could introduce himself.

The boys ate their ramen very quickly that evening and left for home a lot earlier than usual. Neither of them was in a happy mood and they were both looking forward to a good night's sleep.

Shin had been in Tokyo for less than twelve months and being an egotistical and self-absorbed person, he'd never bothered to get to know the other people who worked at his new office. If he'd asked questions about Ami, the office lady who he did his very best to avoid, he would have discovered she was very popular with the others on the team and she was well-respected for her hard work and sweet personality. Ami was also a keen sportswoman and a competitive tennis player. Two years earlier, she'd fractured her ankle during an intense game of doubles and she'd had to wear a cast for six weeks and for a further thirty-six weeks she'd been forced to take it easy and stay off her feet as much as possible. During this time Ami had put on ten kilos in weight and she'd needed to buy a whole new set of work clothes to compensate for her weight gain. After a successful course of sports rehabilitation, Ami had returned to playing tennis competitively and she'd rapidly lost the weight that she'd gained after the accident. Ami had not had the time to go out and buy new clothes for work and although she knew her office outfits were too big, she had every intention of getting new clothes when she'd finished making the repayments on a new car she'd purchased three years earlier. Ami was also very short-sighted and she had to wear thick glasses to ensure that she always read the numbers correctly at work. Ami did own contact lenses but they sometimes irritated her eyes and she'd only wear them on nights out and on dates.

When Shin had started working at the office, Ami had developed a small crush on him but as the months progressed she'd gradually lost interest in him due to his arrogant nature. When Ami was introduced to Ryota, she'd instantly fallen head over heels in love with him instead. Ryota became the centre of her world and he was just as fascinated with her. Ami continued to be polite and as nice as she could be to Shin as it was not in her nature to be rude to anyone.

Shin was completely disinterested in other people's lives and mostly unaware of any other social interactions in the office. When Shin had received the expensive chocolates from Ami on Valentine's Day, he'd not noticed that four of the other men in the office had also received a box from Ami but Ryota had actually received a large basket of chocolates from her. Ami had no idea that Shin believed she had a crush on him as she was very involved with Ryota but some of the other boys in the office thought it might be a bit of fun to make Shin believe that Ami was in love with him, knowing Shin would eventually discover that Ami was dating Ryota.

* * *

The weather in the first week of April was very chilly and the cherry blossoms in Tokyo arrived a little later than usual, however by the middle of the month they were in full bloom and their pink and white petals were lining the streets, creating a prettiness that deserved full appreciation. At just after eight p.m. on the second Friday of the month, the evening lights reflected off each bud and flower giving them a soft and attractive glow. Despite the heavenly surroundings, Shin was frustrated and unhappy when he met with Kenta at their favourite yatai mobile food station in Sakura-Shinmachi for their monthly catch up.

'I've made a big mistake – I'm an idiot,' were Shin's first words as he sat down on the wobbly wooden stool next to his friend.

'What's the matter?' asked Kenta, worried by the expression on Shin's face that he might have made a huge mistake at work or he'd lost a lot of money.

'She's beautiful and now I'll never be able to take her out because of the way I've treated her,' said Shin.

'Who do you think is beautiful?' asked Kenta. He'd had a very busy day at his office and he hadn't seen or spoken to his friend for four weeks. He had no idea who Shin was talking about. Many girls had come and gone over the years and it was sometimes difficult to keep up with all the women Shin mentioned.

'Ami-san – she's gorgeous, smart and funny and she's going out with Ryota-kun and completely ignoring me. She should break up with him and give me a chance to get to know her better,' said Shin.

Kenta was perplexed and surprised at Shin's sudden change of heart. 'I thought you said she was ugly and weird looking.'

'Let me explain,' said Shin. 'Everyone in the office went out last night for karaoke to celebrate the general manager's birthday and Ami-san was there,' said Shin, throwing back his glass of shōchū before holding up his empty glass to the owner who gave him a refill. 'I didn't recognise her at first because she wasn't wearing her uniform, her hair wasn't tied back and those thick, black glasses that don't do her any justice were nowhere to be seen. When we arrived at the karaoke box, Ami-san sat down next to me on the sofa and Ryota-kun was sitting on the other side of her. She completely turned her back to me and she didn't say a word to me all evening. When Ryota-kun stood up to sing a rendition of *All You Need is Love* by The Beatles in English, I thought I'd have a chance to talk to her but instead she called over one of the office ladies and spent the whole time telling her how much she liked Ryota-kun. I spent the whole night not talking with anyone. I just watched the back of Ami-san's head or her beautiful profile without sharing a single word with her. At about nine thirty p.m., I announced to the whole group that I'd had enough, I was really tired and I wanted to go home but my general manager gave me a look which basically said don't you dare disrespect me by leaving early, so I changed my mind and I had to spend another hour and a half waiting until everybody else was ready to leave.

I ended up listening the whole time to Ryota-kun and Ami-san flirt with each other while everyone else ignored me. I kept wishing Ami-san would turn around and flirt with me as well, now that I've discovered how pretty and how nice she is. I've been thinking about her all day today and I've realised I really like her. Ami-san is captivating, she's alluring and she's everything I've been looking for in a woman and now I don't have a chance to get to know her because I've been stupid and I've ignored her advances for months.'

'That's such a pity,' said Kenta. He was worried about Shin but he couldn't help feeling a bit victorious that his much better-looking friend had finally met his match and Shin didn't get exactly who or whatever he wanted for a change.

'Maybe I was too quick to judge,' said Shin, quickly downing his second glass of shōchū before requesting yet another, even before he'd had a chance to try the ramen which had just been placed in front of him.

'Maybe it wasn't meant to be,' said Kenta, thinking more about how delicious his first mouthful of ramen tasted rather than concentrating on his friend's problem.

'Oh, I'm going to get very drunk tonight,' said Shin – and that's exactly what he did.

My Coming of Age Disaster

My Coming of Age Day was approaching. This would be a significant occasion for me and at twenty years old I'd finally become an adult. My mother and I had been talking about this day for about two years and as I was a traditionalist I'd been dreaming for many years more about how exciting it would be, what I would wear and how I'd feel on the day.

Tomorrow would be the second Monday in January and the day I'd take my giant and momentous step into adulthood. From tomorrow, I'd be able to vote, purchase alcohol or marry without my parents' consent if I so wished. I considered myself to be a person who had a huge respect and admiration for my country and the Japanese culture and it had always been in my nature to embrace the charming and very beautiful aspects of our customs in Japan. Ikebana flower arrangement and classes in tea ceremony had been passions of mine since childhood and I've forever been applauded by my elders for the way in which I was so determined to preserve and maintain our national identity. My mother had always instilled in me a belief that our ethnicity should never be overlooked, as my focus and that of my peers was swept away by the distractions of everyday life and the temptations of youth.

My family and friends also knew how much I adored pretty dresses, shiny jewellery, colourful art and eye-catching creations. Pink was my favourite colour but I also liked anything designed in pastel hues or something covered all over in ornate flowers and intricate patterns. My bedroom was filled with Japanese and Western dolls and I loved to hang pictures of figurines in traditional kimonos on the wall above my bed. I'd just started wearing make-up and although I preferred a natural look, I often wore a shiny pink lip-gloss and a soft plum blusher whenever I went out. I never dyed my hair because my jet black bob with my very thick, straight and heavy fringe was the hairstyle that suited me best. The ebony colour of my tresses kept my complexion looking fresh and other people often said to me that my beauty had a timeless quality that I should never consider changing.

Sometimes in the evening when my father arrived home from work, he would join in the discussions about my imminent Coming of Age Day which my mother and I could talk about for hours. My twin brother Saburo always ignored us as he sat and watched television in the corner of the living room. Saburo considered himself to be too advanced and modern-minded to be involved in the Coming of Age ceremony. He liked to dye his hair a deep purple and he wore punkish denim jackets covered all over in silver studs. The first thing you noticed when you opened our front door was my brother's Dr Martens boots with yellow laces at the entrance to our home, lined up in defiance next to the rest of our plain and much more conservative shoes. Saburo embraced his individuality and he always liked to remind us that he was different.

I could tell he truly believed he was more evolved than the rest of us. He would occasionally shout out from his position in front of the television in the living room that I was old-fashioned and out-of-touch with reality, but my parents and I would ignore him and we'd continue to discuss kimono patterns and hairstyles for my important day.

I went to sleep on the second Sunday in January wondering how my friends would look in their furisode kimonos and I woke up several times during the night brimming with anticipation.

My mother came to wake me the following morning and I could tell by the look on her face as I opened my eyes that she was just as pleased as me that my Coming of Age Day had finally arrived. I was unable to eat even one bite at breakfast but I did manage to drink several cups of green tea to calm my nerves.

My brother's friends Yori and Nori arrived at our home before my mother and I left to take care of our preparations in town. The boys went straight to Saburo's room with a box of Asahi Super Dry beers without even saying hello to me. Yori and Nori both wore similar studded denim jackets and scowls on their faces just like my brother. They also dyed their hair a variety of offbeat colours.

In the past couple of days, my parents and I were so disappointed to hear my brother repeatedly say that the Coming of Age Day ceremony was a waste of time and there was no chance he'd adhere to the standards of a group of archaic officials. He also told us he wasn't prepared to sit through a succession of long and boring speeches which he thought would have no relevance to his life now or in the future. My parents and I knew

Saburo could be very stubborn and if he chose to ignore this important day we would have to accept his decision.

I'd planned to meet with my friends Manami and Wakana later that morning but first my mother and I made our way to the shop that hired out the furisode kimonos. The ladies who worked there could see we were brimming with excitement. They seemed to really enjoy their job and they were full of compliments as they helped me tie my kimono. After this my mother and I planned to make our way to the beauty salon to have my hair and make-up carefully applied.

One hour later, my mother and I left the kimono hire shop where I'd been dressed by an expert in a modern pale pink furisode kimono covered in cherry blossoms with a matching obi sash tied neatly under my bust. This was the very first time I'd ever worn a kimono fit for an adult and although it was a little difficult to walk in the white tabi-socks and the zori-sandals, I really felt this transformation into a full-sleeved kimono truly marked my journey into adulthood in a way that felt spiritual and fulfilling.

My mother and I walked the short distance from the hire shop to the beauty parlour. The morning air was frosty and I was glad I had a white fur shawl to cover my shoulders. The cold weather and my nervousness on this special day made me shudder and twice I felt a chill run down the back of my neck. Despite this, I hoped I'd look back on this day with a sense of nostalgia and contentment.

The ladies at the beauty parlour were very professional when it came to setting hair and applying make-up for the young girls celebrating their Coming of Age Day and it took them just under an hour to complete my

transformation. I was delighted with the result and when I twirled my chair around and stood up to present myself to my waiting mother, I was sure I could see tears in her eyes. Her reaction confirmed in my heart that everything looked as perfect as it should be.

My father had a close friend who was a professional photographer. Later that morning before I had to leave for the big event, he came over to see us and take some formal photos of me as a personal favour to my family. I felt like an empress for the day as I posed next to the pond and under the Gingko biloba tree in our garden. My parents joined me for a few of these photos but I didn't ask my brother nor did I want him to join us for these moments which were captured in time forever more. A short while later, my father drove me to the ceremony looking the proudest I'd ever seen him. He couldn't stop grinning as he escorted his only daughter in all her finery to this special event and it was hard to say goodbye to him when he stopped the car to let me out. As I stepped onto the curb, I wished for a moment that my brother had cleaned up his act and he was standing there beside me, but I knew he was dead set against all this pomp and pageantry and it was now too late for him to change his mind.

My friends Manami and Wakana came scuttling towards me as I adjusted my kimono and said goodbye to my father. Manami looked very sweet although a little outdated in a pale blue furisode kimono which she'd borrowed from her mother who'd worn the same kimono at her own Coming of Age Day many years before. Wakana, in complete contrast, looked enviably magnificent in the most beautiful kimono I'd ever seen. I'd heard from Manami that Wakana had bought her furisode kimono from a department store in Ginza and the difference in the quality of her silk kimono was outstanding. Wakana's shoulders were draped in the prettiest rich peach colour above the obi sash and below the sash her torso and her long swinging sleeves were covered with a very tasteful and intricate pattern of hand-painted plum blossoms. Manami had told me Wakana's parents had paid more than ¥1,000,000 for their daughter's furisode kimono but I knew she'd be able to wear it to lots of other parties and to her friends' weddings until she became a married woman, as would I if I owned such a stunning kimono. Dressed in such luxury and good taste, Wakana was receiving lots of attention from the girls standing around us and I almost didn't want to stand next to her in the fear that I might look shabby in comparison. I reminded myself I had to spend the rest of the day with Wakana. She was throwing a party at her house later and we'd be joined by dozens of others who were marking the day and its celebration. I was really looking forward to this. After the lengthy speeches it would be great to have a few drinks and sing some karaoke.

We shuffled into the auditorium, commenting on the kimonos worn by the girls who were standing in groups beside us or nearby. A few minutes later, Manami, Wakana and I had just started debating on whether the boys looked better in a suit and tie or in a traditional dark kimono, hakama and haori, when we realised the officials were about to start their speeches. Just as the noise around us began to subside and the officials took their place on the stage, we could hear screams coming from the left of us which made us all turn around. I craned my neck to see what all the commotion was about and I could just make out three punks, drunk and stumbling towards the stage, holding tubes of Kewpie mayonnaise in their hands which they'd begun to squirt at the officials. I couldn't see the faces on these riotous boys but I was glad to see several policemen rushing forward ready to apprehend them.

Manami, Wakana and I were at the back of the room near the exit. We knew the policemen would have to escort the delinquents past us to take them out for an arrest. I nearly fainted when the policemen approached us, pushing the three boys. I recognised with shock and horror the faces of my brother Saburo and his friends Yori and Nori and I cringed as I watched them yelling and screaming as the policemen tried to lead them by the arm out of the building. I tried to move back towards the corner of this expansive room, pulling Manami and Wakana with me in the hope they would not recognise my brother, but just before the policemen reached the exit I saw my brother break free and I felt my knees go weak as I watched him running and pushing through the crowds towards where we were standing as he tried to escape. Saburo saw me stamping my foot with frustration and displeasure as our eyes met. My brother threw back his head and guffawed like a crazy man as he ran about and squirted mayonnaise up and down and left and right, revelling in the fact he'd managed to completely humiliate me and create a major disturbance at the ceremony. Unfortunately for Wakana, she was straight in front of Saburo's line of fire and she ended up with oily mayonnaise stains all down the left-hand side of her expensive kimono. Wakana naturally broke into a fit of tears and I knew the whole day was spoiled and a chance that we'd be partying later at Wakana's home was now completely ruined. I took hold of my brother's arm and with a strength which I didn't know I possessed I pushed Saburo back into the waiting arms of the closest policeman. I turned to Wakana and apologised profusely. Luckily for me, she was a very kind and humble friend and she didn't blame me for my brother's terrible deed.

I watched my brother being led away to a waiting police van as I rushed out of the auditorium to call my parents from my mobile phone. My father answered the phone and he was livid when he heard about how Saburo had brought so much shame upon our family. My father was an honourable man and I was not surprised when he promised to pay for any damage to Wakana's kimono and when he told me how sorry he was that Saburo had ruined such an important day for us. I could only speak briefly to my father as tears were streaming down my face, but my father promised to come quickly to pick me up before other people came out of the auditorium wanting to discuss with me what had happened with my brother and his friends. I couldn't go back inside where Wakana was being comforted by Manami and a few of the other girls, now understandably terribly upset that her beautiful kimono was so badly stained. I felt more shame and humiliation than I'd ever felt before. If these feelings were an indication of what it was like to be an adult, I would have preferred a much more romantic alternative.

THE END

Thank you for reading

TOKYO TALES: A COLLECTION
OF JAPANESE SHORT STORIES

By Renae Lucas-Hall

Illustrations by Yoshimi OHTANI

....

The research for this book was facilitated by

Goodman, R., Imoto, Y. and Toivonen, T. (2012)
A Sociology of Japanese Youth,
USA and Canada: Nissan Institute/Routledge
Japanese Studies Series

....

Find out more about the author Renae Lucas-Hall, her
books and her writing at http://www.renaelucashall.com

Enjoy more images by the Japanese Illustrator
Yoshimi OHTANI at
http://ARTas1.com/yoshimi_ohtani

If you enjoyed *Tokyo Tales: A Collection of Japanese Short Stories*, you'll love *Tokyo Hearts: A Japanese Love Story* by Renae Lucas-Hall.
Visit **http://www.renaelucashall.com** to find out more.

TOKYO HEARTS: A JAPANESE LOVE STORY by **RENAE LUCAS-HALL**

Tokyo Hearts is a poignant love story that will catapult you directly onto the fashionable streets of Japan's capital and into the hearts of Takashi and Haruka.

Takashi is a young and popular university student who has fallen in love with his stylish and sophisticated friend Haruka. She is sweet and kind and adores shopping for high-end Japanese and Western brands.

Every week, they meet up in the heart of Tokyo, enjoying each other's company, and for Takashi, life is perfect. However, the path to true love is never easy. When Takashi discovers that Haruka is seeing her wealthy ex-boyfriend from Kyoto, his life begins to turn upside down.

This coming of age story traces the lives of Takashi and Haruka and their friends as they deal with young love and the ups and downs of growing up in Tokyo – truly one of the most stylish, energetic and exhilarating cities in the world.

....

"For us at TripFiction, this is a fabulous novel that weaves its way into the heart of Tokyo life and brings the city into sharp focus for the reader…If you fancy an armchair trip to Tokyo, either to rekindle memories of a visit, or to prepare for an upcoming journey; or just because you want a bit of insight, then give this book a go." – TripFiction